Buried Secrets

As Lilia's fingers touched the stone, Lex brushed her hand with his. He'd hoped to hold her hand, to feel the softness of her touch. Instead, he watched, horrified, as her eyes suddenly rolled back in her head.

"My father . . . ," Lilia intoned in a low, guttural voice. "I hate my father . . . I hate him, hate him; why, why does he have to come here? What does he want from me? Why can't he just love me? Why can't he just love me the way that Clark's parents love him? Why —"

Lex was stunned. Lilia looked like she was having some kind of seizure, her eyes rolled far back in her head, her body stiff with shock. But she was talking. Her voice was rambling, narrating a stream of consciousness. They weren't her thoughts, though, Lex realized with mounting alarm. They were his . . .

My God, Lex thought. She's reading my mind.

SMALLVILLE™

Available from Little, Brown and Company

SMALLVILLE™

Buried Secrets

Suzan Colón

**Superman created by
Jerry Siegel and Joe Shuster**

LITTLE, BROWN AND COMPANY

New York ❧ An AOL Time Warner Company

For Mom and Dad, who rock;
for Steve Korté, who is a great editor and friend;
and for Francesco Clark, who really is a super man.

First Edition

The characters and events portrayed in this book are
fictitious. Any similarity to real persons, living or dead, is
coincidental and not intended by the author.

Library of Congress Cataloging-in-Publication Data

Colón, Suzan.
    Smallville : buried secrets / by Suzan Colón.
        p. cm. — (Smallville ; #6)
    Summary: Clark Kent, who will later be known as Super-
man, has a crush on the new Spanish teacher at his high
school — and so does Lex Luthor who, when he discovers
that she can read minds, is determined to find out what she
knows about Clark's secret.
    ISBN 0-316-16848-3
    [1. Extrasensory perception — Fiction.   2. Interpersonal
relations — Fiction.   3. Heroes — Fiction.]   I. Smallville
(Television program)   II. Title.   III. Series.

PZ7.C71637Sm 2003
[Fic] — dc21   2002040705

10 9 8 7 6 5 4 3 2 1

Q-BF

Printed in the United States of America

Prologue

Smallville, Kansas, 1989

It was one of the most gorgeous days anyone in Smallville could remember. It was like a picture on a postcard: the skies were incredibly blue and clear; the sun shone down on everything below and made the cornfields look like green silk; a gentle breeze rippled a nearby pond. It was a perfect day for a picnic.

"Beautiful out here, no?" said a man to his wife. "Nothing but fresh air, sunshine, and land." His wife continued to make sandwiches and said nothing. "Carmen," he said, touching her arm. "Please. Just look at it."

She looked out in the same direction as her husband, but what she saw was quite different. Flat, endless fields of nothing. The only part of the landscape she was moved by was her nine-year-old daughter, who was busily kicking a soccer ball in the grass. But she kept these thoughts to herself.

"Aren't we on Luthor property?" she said. "Or is this still your father's land?"

"It's still my father's land — the pond divides the two. Tell me, Carmen, honestly," the man said, turning toward his wife, "do you like it here any better now?"

Carmen hoped her smile didn't look too forced. "*Sí*, José, much better," she lied.

"I know Smallville isn't as exciting as Madrid, Carmencita," José said. "I know you miss your teaching job at the university there. But you remember when we were first married, I said I'd want to return home someday? To farm the land, as my father did?"

Carmen was nodding. "*Sí, sí*, José. I remember. And I agreed we could come here, didn't I? It has been an adjustment, yes. But I know you love it here."

José sighed, relieved. He'd thought that Carmen wouldn't like living in Smallville. But when his father left him the family farm — acres and acres of lush cornfields — he'd jumped at the chance to leave his boring office job at an insurance company and return home. Now, a year later, his wife said she was happy, and his daughter seemed to love Smallville as much as he did. He smiled as he watched her kick the ball farther into the field.

"Lilia," Carmen called, "don't go too far."

"Relax," her husband said. "What could happen to her here?"

🐱 🐱 🐱 🐱

Lilia Sanchez didn't hear her parents. She was concentrating hard on keeping the ball in play. Having lived in Madrid for the first eight years of her life, she'd been brought up watching soccer on TV and playing it in school. It wasn't as popular here in the United States as it was in Europe — yet. But she had been talking to her gym teacher, who had said that if enough of Lilia's classmates were interested, she would start a soccer team. And Lilia wanted to be ready.

Got to keep my knees high, she thought. *And kick, and GOOOOAAAL! The crowd goes wild! Lilia Sanchez scores again!*

At that moment, Lilia heard what sounded like thunder. In Kansas, thunderstorms could be pretty scary — the skies went black, thunder made the house shudder, and lightning struck the fields. But when Lilia looked at the sky, she saw no clouds. Only fire.

❧ ❧ ❧ ❧

"Lilia!" Carmen was screaming. "Lilia, *run!*"

Carmen and José had never seen anything like what was happening. They'd heard the distant rumblings and also thought it was a storm coming in. But when they looked up, they saw huge balls of fire hurtling toward the earth.

The first meteorite hit a cornfield a mile away. Carmen and José felt the ground shake beneath them from the impact and saw flames and smoke shoot up above the cornfield. Then another meteorite landed, closer to town. More explosions.

Carmen was screaming. José looked out into the field; his daughter had fallen down and was transfixed by shock.

"Lilia!" he shouted. "Get to the car!"

Quickly, Lilia scrambled to her feet. A small flaming meteorite plunged into the field. The explosion knocked her back to the ground. Again, she got up and headed to her parents.

Carmen was running toward her daughter in a panic. She watched as a tiny meteorite shot down from the sky . . . right toward Lilia.

"*No!*" she screamed as the meteorite struck the ground just a few feet behind Lilia. It exploded on impact, sending Lilia flying.

"*Dios mío*," Carmen prayed. "Please, God, let her be all right." She was the first to reach her daughter, and she took her in her arms. Tiny shards of meteorite were all around her, glowing hot and green. José was at their side a split second later. "Lilia! Lilia, are you hurt?"

Lilia's father cradled her head; tiny streaks of blood wet his hand, but she didn't seem to be badly injured. Lilia moaned, and her eyelids fluttered. "Oh, thank heaven," her father said as Carmen held Lilia in her arms, making soothing noises.

Then, suddenly, Lilia spoke. But the way she spoke was very different from the way she usually did. It sounded, José thought later, as if someone else was speaking through her.

"I hate this place . . . ," Lilia intoned. Her eyes were now open, rolled back in her head, and she sounded serious, angry. *"I hate being a farmer's wife! I was a teacher in Madrid; we were happy there. Why couldn't you just stay in the insurance office? I never wanted to come here! I hate this godforsaken flatland, and now look, look what has happened to our daughter. I hate Smallville; I hate it. I HATE IT —"*

CHAPTER 1

Smallville 2003

Clark! Hey, son, can you give me a hand here?"

Clark Kent looked up from his homework. He was in the barn hayloft, where his father had put some old comfy furniture, a table, and Clark's telescope. It was a little extra space for Clark to sit, think, hang out; his father liked to call it his "Fortress of Solitude." Clark stuck his head out the large window to see his dad in front of the tractor, which had an obvious flat.

"Be right there," he called back.

Jonathan Kent, Clark's father, was holding a broken jack. "I knew this old thing was going to go sooner or later," he sighed, shaking his head. "Son, do you mind . . . ?"

Clark smiled. "No sweat, Dad." He leaned over

and, without the slightest sign of strain, lifted the back of the tractor off the ground.

Jonathan knelt by the wheel and began working at the tire bolts with a wrench. "It's okay, Dad, I'll do it," Clark said. His father smiled and watched as his sixteen-year-old son unscrewed each two-inch bolt with his fingertips, just spinning them around as though they'd already been loosened by an electric wrench. Balancing the tractor on his shoulder, Clark removed the huge flat tire and tossed it aside as though it were a bicycle tire. Jonathan struggled to roll the new one over to Clark, who pushed it on easily and screwed the bolts back in place in seconds.

"That okay?" he said to his father.

"Let's see," Jonathan said.

Clark let the tractor go, sliding its two tons gently off his shoulder. He pushed it back and forth, making sure the tire held fast. His father was chuckling.

"I'm sure glad you can do that," Jonathan said, clapping his son on the back, "and that you can do it fast." He glanced up the road that led to the house.

Clark turned to see what his father was looking at, and he broke out into a grin. Jogging up the road was Lana Lang, the girl who lived on the property next to the Kent Farm and who was one of Clark's closest friends.

Close, he thought, *but not as close as I'd like.* He waved to Lana, and she waved back as she headed up the road to the Kent house.

"Try not to do anything like that in front of Lana, okay, son?" Jonathan said, only half-joking.

"No problem," Clark said. "All my energy usually goes into trying not to blow my cool in front of her, anyway."

Jonathan waved to Lana as he got on the tractor and drove toward the vegetable fields. "Hi, Mr. Kent," Lana called as she jogged past him, then began walking over to Clark.

Only Lana Lang, Clark thought, could look beautiful in sweatpants, no makeup, and with her hair tied back in a ponytail. She had an incredible smile that made her almond eyes look even more exotic than they usually did. Whenever that smile was directed toward Clark, as it was now, he felt like he could fly.

"Hey," he said.

"Hi," she said. "Are you busy?"

"Nope." He shrugged. "Just finished helping my dad change a tire. What's up?"

"I was kind of hoping I could talk to you about something," Lana said, her expression becoming a little more serious.

❧ ❧ ❧ ❧

Clark led Lana up to his place in the hayloft. With its big window it was sort of like being outside, and it had an excellent view of the sunset, which was now coloring the whole barn in brilliant gold and scarlet hues. Besides, Clark thought, it would be weird to bring Lana to his bedroom. It would feel a little too intimate, considering the fact that she had a boyfriend.

Whitney Fordman had been a thorn in Clark's side ever since Clark had gotten to high school. Whitney was a popular jock who set out to make Clark's life miserable after he realized that Clark had a crush on his girlfriend. Not that Clark was any lightweight; he was just as big as Whitney. But considering the unusual level of strength Clark had, he didn't dare fight with him — not even after Whitney and his fellow football goons had tied Clark to a post in a field like a scarecrow, his chest spray-painted with a big red *S*, as a prank.

They would never have been able to do anything like that to Clark if Whitney hadn't wrapped Lana's necklace around Clark's neck. It was meant to be an insult, but for Clark it caused real injury; the necklace had a small green meteorite fragment on it. Lana used to wear it in memory of her parents, who were killed in the meteorite shower that hit Smallville fourteen years ago. The translucent green meteorites, which glowed eerily whenever Clark was near them, were the only things that could hurt Clark, as far as he and his parents knew. Just being near one could bring him to his knees.

But, strangely, things with Whitney had turned around. First, he had been humbled by the loss of his football scholarship. Then, his father had passed away. Clark had seen Whitney in a different way at the funeral, and Whitney apparently felt somehow changed too. After his father's death, he suddenly enlisted in the Marines.

There was an official stamp — USMC, for United States Marine Corps — on the letter that Lana now held in her hand.

"I got a letter from Whitney," she said simply.

Clark felt ashamed because he immediately wished Whitney had written that he was breaking up with Lana. He had been hoping that Whitney's absence would clear the way for him and Lana to be together. She had even given Whitney her meteorite necklace as something to remember her by, so now Clark didn't feel sick when Lana was around him.

Somehow, though, things hadn't happened the way he wanted them to. Now, maybe . . . Clark waited for Lana to sit down and continue.

"He said some things in here that I may be reading into too much," Lana said. "I was wondering if I could get a guy's perspective."

"Sure," Clark said.

"I'll just skip to the parts I don't understand," Lana said, and then she read aloud: " 'I'm sorry I had to leave so quickly, and I know you were confused about things when I left. I remember saying "I love you," and I realized later that you never said it back . . .' "

Here it comes, Clark thought. His heart began to thud in his chest. He'd adored Lana for so long . . . Was this finally his chance?

" 'But in my heart,' " Lana continued, " 'I know you have feelings for me, even if you're not sure what they are. And I know that you and I are meant to be together, forever. There's a bond between us that can't be broken, and I see a beautiful future for us.' " Lana paused for a second to take a breath. " 'And when we're together again, something will happen that will make you realize that too.' " She swallowed and folded the letter, looking at Clark.

He was completely confused. Whitney hadn't said anything at all about breaking up with Lana. Why did she look so upset?

"I — I don't understand," Clark finally said.

"I guess what I'm asking you," Lana said, "is whether you think Whitney is . . . proposing."

"Proposing what?" Clark asked, not willing to go there.

"Marriage," Lana said.

Clark's heart sank. *This can't be happening*, he thought. Lana couldn't possibly be telling him that she was going to marry Whitney. He got up and turned his back so Lana couldn't see the shocked look he was sure he had on his face.

"Whoa," was all he could think of to say. "Uh . . . that's pretty heavy."

"Do you think that's what it is?" Lana asked. "I mean, am I misunderstanding what Whitney's saying? I could be making this huge mistake." She laughed weakly.

Marrying Whitney would *be a huge mistake*, Clark thought. He still couldn't bring himself to say anything. The words couldn't make it past the huge knot in his throat.

He'd been in love with Lana forever. He'd even had a crush on her when they were little kids. She'd treated him like a brother then, but just this past year, his friendship with her had deepened, become closer and more meaningful. *We have a special bond, not Lana and Whitney,* Clark thought.

"It's not that I don't have feelings for Whitney," Lana said. "I do, or I wouldn't be with him, would I?" Clark took the question as rhetorical. If he hadn't been so upset, he would have realized that Lana was really asking herself.

"It's just that . . . I mean, love —," Lana said, "you can't just say that to anyone. You really have to mean it, and you have to know what it means." Out of the corner of his eye, Clark could see Lana begin to pace back and forth slowly, as if she was trying to work something out. He couldn't bring himself to look at her, and he wasn't really hearing her, either.

"I don't know," she said plaintively. "I'm not even sure if I know what love is." She was struggling now and clearly needed something. Something that Clark, at the moment, couldn't give her.

I know what love is, he thought bitterly. *And right now it hurts.*

"Clark," she said, standing in front of him. "Do you . . . have you . . . ever been confused about your feelings for someone?"

Now Clark turned to Lana and looked deep into her eyes, yet he still couldn't see the pleading look in them. Her eyes were so beautiful. Bullets couldn't hurt him, but at that moment Lana's eyes were breaking his heart.

"No," Clark said, his jaw set. "I've always known exactly what my feelings were."

☙ ☙ ☙ ☙

Clark ran. He ran as fast as he could, and to a human being's eye he was just a high-speed blur of motion.

After Lana left, Clark had tried to pretend that he was all right, to just go back to doing his homework. That worked for about five seconds, and then his frustration had boiled to the top and he'd slammed his book shut. He'd looked out the window to make sure no one was around to see him, then jumped out of the hayloft, landed on his feet two stories below, and took off running.

It was the only thing he could think of to do to burn off this awful feeling. He was mad at Lana for reading him Whitney's letter, mad at her for being with Whitney in the first place, and most of all mad at himself. Lana had come to Clark not to rub his nose in anything but to get a friend's advice. *And I acted like a jerk,* he thought.

Clark realized he might be Lana's closest friend. She was one of the most popular girls at school, always surrounded by people. But once, she had told Clark that she felt as if only he saw who she really was. And he'd told her he felt the same way.

Then why can't she see that I'm in love with her? he thought, finally coming to a halt on the dusty road. Though hardly anything strained him, even he was winded from running so fast and so far. He looked around and guessed he was about sixty or so miles from his house.

For a while, Clark had been content with Lana's friendship. Probably, he admitted to himself, because he'd thought that eventually it would become more than a friendship. To Clark, he and Lana made a much better pair than she and Whitney.

Sure, they made sense on the surface. After all, Whitney had been the captain of the football team, and Lana had been head cheerleader. But if you scratched a little deeper, it didn't add up. Whitney had been happy just to be a jock; Lana had quit cheerleading because she found more important things to do, like persuading Lex Luthor to finance the restoration of the old Talon movie theater, where Lana's parents first met. Lana was deep, thoughtful, sensitive. Clark was —

Just her sidekick, he thought. *That's all I'm ever going to be to Lana.* Frustrated, he picked up a stone and hurled it at the ground, sending it six feet down into the earth.

CHAPTER 2

By the time he got to school the next day, Clark had gone over what had happened with Lana a dozen times, and each time he had a different solution. First, he wanted to run to her and apologize. Then, he thought maybe she owed him an apology. No, that didn't seem right . . . Maybe this was just the way things were going to be, and they were going to go their separate ways, once and for all . . .

"Clark, man, are you even listening to me?" said Pete Ross, waving his hand across Clark's face to break his daydreamy spell. "Hel-*lo*, Earth to Clark . . ."

"Sorry, Pete," Clark said as they walked along the school hallway, which was crowded with kids going to their next classes. "What did you say?"

Pete sighed, mock annoyed at his friend. "I was saying that we've got a new Spanish teacher."

"Really?" Clark said. "What happened to Mr. Hector?"

"You mean *Señor* Hector," Pete said with exaggeration. "Didn't you hear? He's off for three weeks on a sabbatical or something. Personally, I think he just ran screaming at the thought of trying to get those verbs into my head for one more semester." Clark laughed as he put his books in his locker, but Pete shook his head. "I'm serious, man. If I don't bring my Spanish grades up, I'm looking at summer school. And my dad is not going to be down with that."

"Don't worry, Pete. You'll do okay," Clark said, putting a hand on his friend's shoulder. "Let's go check out who's torturing us instead of Mister — er, *Señor* Hector."

☞ ☞ ☞ ☞

When Clark and Pete walked into their Spanish class, there was a young woman writing on the chalkboard — PROFESORA LILIA SANCHEZ. She was petite, with straight, glossy dark hair that swung gently around her shoulders as she moved. She was wearing a red sweater and a white skirt with roses on it. It was a pretty cute outfit for a teacher, more like something a student would wear. Then she put down the chalk, turned around, and . . .

Wow, Clark thought.

The teacher couldn't have been more than twenty-three or twenty-four, younger than any of his other teachers at Smallville High. And she was totally gorgeous. She looked kind of like Penelope Cruz and Jennifer Lopez morphed together.

"*Hola,*" she said to Clark and Pete.

"Oh, uh — I mean, *hola,*" Clark stammered. He was vaguely aware of Pete snickering behind him, but not really. Clark didn't realize he was just standing there staring until the teacher, this beautiful woman, spoke again.

"*Me llamo Profesora Sanchez,*" she said, walking toward them. "*¿Y usted?*"

"Yo, Clark," Pete whispered. "I think she's asking what your name is."

In truth, Clark understood exactly what she was saying. He generally didn't have problems with Spanish, or with any other subject for that matter. He didn't know if he did well in school because of his special powers, but the fact that he could read a textbook in under a minute probably didn't hurt. However, right now he couldn't think, and he was even feeling a little lightheaded — something that rarely happened to a guy who could take a bullet in the chest and live to talk about it at dinnertime.

All of this happened in just a few seconds, but to Clark it felt as if everything around him was in slow motion, like when he went into superspeed mode. But when Clark heard someone else chuckle, he snapped out of it. "Uh, *me llamo* Clark Kent," he answered, thinking he'd better get to his desk. He vaguely heard Pete introduce himself in halting Spanish.

"*Sientense, por favor.*" The teacher smiled. "Sit down, please, and let's begin."

At dinner that night, Clark's father interrupted a story he was telling when he noticed his son had a slight smile on his face.

"I didn't think fertilizer was that amusing," Jonathan said jokingly.

Clark looked up. "I'm sorry, Dad. What were you saying?"

"I think you probably had a much more interesting day than I did," Jonathan said, reaching for the salad. "Something good happen at school today?"

Clark's smile went from sixty to a hundred watts in a flash. "Um . . . you could say that," he replied.

Jonathan and Martha just looked at each other and smiled, thinking the same thing: it had to have something to do with Lana Lang. But apparently, Clark wasn't ready to tell them about it just yet.

"Is there any more meat loaf, Mom?" he asked innocently.

☙ ☙ ☙ ☙

"Clark, man, what's the rush?" Pete said, trying to keep up with his friend. "It's only Spanish class, not a free trip to the moon."

"I just don't want to be late, that's all," Clark said, slowing down a little. The truth was, he couldn't wait to get to Spanish now that Ms. Sanchez was there. It was only her third day at the school, but Clark had to admit (only to himself) that he was developing a major crush on her.

Clark's thoughts were interrupted when someone accidentally bumped into him in the crowded hallway; it was Daniel Huang, another student in Clark and Pete's Spanish class.

"Oh, sorry, Clark," Daniel said. "I didn't see you."

"That's okay," Clark said, watching as Daniel headed down the hall toward the classroom. Clark turned to Pete. "He looked kind of upset."

Pete nodded. "I thought I was bugging about Spanish, but he's really flipping," he said. "It's the only subject he's having trouble with, and it's bringing his grade point average down. His parents aren't too thrilled. I can totally relate, but he's getting really nervous about report card time."

Daniel was studying his Spanish book intently when Clark and Pete walked into the classroom and sat down. Ms. Sanchez was writing the day's lesson on the chalkboard, her back to the students; in the middle of writing out a sentence, she turned around and walked over to Daniel's desk. Though she whispered, Clark could hear her ask if Daniel could stay after class to talk. Normally that wasn't what any kid wanted to hear from a teacher, but her smile was gentle, and Daniel seemed to relax.

Later in the class, it was Pete's turn to sweat. The day's assignment was to say in Spanish what your parents did for a living, and Ms. Sanchez had called on Pete. Clark felt for his friend. In addition to Pete's not feeling too confident about his language skills, his family had lost the creamed corn factory they'd owned for years to Lionel Luthor, who had bought it and turned it into a fertilizer plant. Pete's parents had fallen on hard times since then. There was no way Ms. Sanchez could have known this was a doubly embarrassing moment for Pete, who sighed and bravely began: *"Mi padre,* um, *mi padre y . . ."*

Painful seconds went by. Clark tried to give a reassuring look to his friend, who was staring at his fidgeting hands. *"Mi padre . . ."*

"Just take it slowly, *Pedro,"* said Ms. Sanchez gently. "So if what you want to say is 'My father and my uncle owned a corn factory, but —' " She stopped abruptly, then looked sympathetically at Pete, as though she'd suddenly realized something. Then she said, "It's okay, *Pedro.* You can translate another time. How about you, Gina?"

Clark looked at Pete, who was both relieved and confused.

"Did you tell Ms. Sanchez about your family?" Clark asked Pete as they walked to their lockers after class.

"Uh-uh," Pete said. "I don't think she knows anything about that. At first I thought she was just having pity on me, but it was almost like she knew *why* I was sweating it, and she let me off the hook." Pete smiled. "And I don't know if she knew or *how* she knew, but Ms. Sanchez just became my favorite teacher."

❧ ❧ ❧ ❧

"I thought I'd find you here," Clark said to his friend Chloe Sullivan as he walked into the office of the school newspaper.

"Where else would I be?" she said with a slightly harried grin. "It's Thursday, deadline day."

Clark sat down, watching Chloe's fingers fly over her computer's keyboard. "So what's going to be on the front page of this week's *Torch*? Anything interesting?"

"Bad news and bland news," Chloe said, leaning back from the computer screen. "Our top story is that the students won't be getting a week off from school after all because the repair work on the roof is almost done. And the second hot story is that everybody just loves the new substitute Spanish teacher." She exhaled with exasperation.

"Ms. Sanchez?" said Clark, suddenly sitting forward. "You interviewed her?"

"Talk about a slow news week," Chloe said. "Where are the guys who can move objects with their minds and the weird psychotropic flowers that make people go nuts when you need them?"

Chloe, the editor of the newspaper, was already a veteran journalist whose nose for news was much more directed at paranormal events, which were actually pretty normal around Smallville. In her office was what she liked to call the "Wall of Weird," an entire wall full of newspaper clippings about strange events that had happened in and around the town since the meteorite storm.

"So what did Ms. Sanchez say?" Clark asked insistently.

Chloe rolled her eyes. "Not you too," she said.

"Not me too what?"

"Everybody's totally in love with her — mostly guys, obviously," Chloe said. "She's only been here three days and already the kids in her classes are way into her, judging from the quotes I got about her." She turned around to look at Clark, who was now standing behind her so he could see the photo of Ms. Sanchez on Chloe's computer.

The only good thing about Clark's intent focus on the image on her computer, Chloe thought, was that he didn't see the hurt look on her face. She'd had a crush on Clark Kent all last year, even though she knew his heart belonged to Lana Lang. It looked like things were finally going to go her way when Clark had asked her to the junior prom. But that was the night the tornadoes had hit the town, and Clark had run off in the middle of everything to search for Lana. To keep her ego from being bruised any further, Chloe had suggested that she and Clark just stay friends; he'd agreed — very quickly, she remembered with a wince.

And now there was someone else who'd caught Clark's attention. *Sure, everyone but me,* Chloe thought darkly. She tried to comfort herself by reasoning that Clark's friendship was better than nothing. It didn't always work.

"I gather," Chloe said, with the sarcasm that

masked her real feelings, "that I can add you to her list of fans?"

"You could say that," Clark offered, going back to his chair. "I mean, I think she's a really good teacher."

"May I quote you on that?" Chloe smiled. "You're not telling me anything I haven't already heard a dozen times. Oh, and the other quotes I hear over and over are: 'She seems to know exactly what I'm having trouble with' and 'She's totally hot.'"

Clark shrugged and smiled. "It's all true. I'm afraid I can't add anything more interesting to that."

"Actually," — Chloe thought for a second — "Ms. Sanchez *did* have an interesting story."

"If it was interesting to you, there's got to be something strange about it," Clark said.

"I'll ignore that," Chloe said, pushing her blond bangs out of her eyes. "But you're right. Did you know," Chloe began, leaning closer to Clark, "that Ms. Sanchez was almost hit by a meteorite?"

CHAPTER 3

Oh no, Clark thought, *another meteorite story. Please don't let this one be too horrible.*

Clark hated hearing stories of what had happened to people during the meteorite storm that had hit Smallville. There were a lot of those stories, and they almost always involved fear, chaos, destruction, and death. And Clark felt responsible for all of it.

Fiery meteorites weren't the only things heading toward the earth that day. There had also been a small spaceship. In it was a child of about three years old. It was a mystery as to where the spaceship had come from, why the child had been sent, or by whom.

My birth parents, Clark thought. People who

either hadn't wanted him or who had to send him away for some reason. And, if that was the case, people who were probably dead now.

The spaceship and meteorites had rocketed to Earth and crashed in Smallville. Jonathan and Martha Kent had barely managed to swerve their truck out of the path of a huge explosion. The truck had rolled over, and when they came to, they found themselves upside down in the cab looking out at the little boy. He was standing in the middle of a fiery crater, completely unhurt, smiling at them. He had then playfully grabbed the handle of the passenger door and ripped it right off the truck.

Jonathan and Martha, who had prayed for so long for a child, quickly hid the spaceship in their storm cellar and adopted the boy. They named their new son Clark.

He had always known he was adopted, and he'd known he was a little different — the incredible strength, the ability to run faster than any car, and a few recent weird developments, like the sudden ability to see through walls, a kind of X-ray vision. But Clark's parents had told him about the spaceship only last year.

If that hadn't been enough to shake Clark's world, it was nothing compared to how he felt when he realized that he had been part of the disaster that had affected so many people. Lana Lang's parents had been killed in the meteorite shower. Clark's friend Lex Luthor, whose father owned half of Smallville, had been in a cornfield near where a meteorite struck. He'd been inexplicably bald ever since and was extremely self-conscious about it.

And all of it is my fault, Clark thought miserably. Now even Ms. Sanchez, his beautiful Spanish teacher — she was a victim of the meteorite shower too?

"Yep," Chloe was saying. "She came very close to being totally eighty-sixed by a meteorite."

Clark winced. "Tell me what happened," he said.

"Okay, but I'll start from the beginning. As you probably know, Ms. Sanchez comes from Madrid. But her family relocated to Smallville after her grandfather passed away and left the family farm to Ms. Sanchez's father. She was nine then."

"Go on," Clark said, nodding.

"Here's the interesting part. The Sanchezes were out having a picnic when the meteorite shower happened. Ms. Sanchez missed being hit by one by about three feet. Apparently it shattered on impact right behind her."

Clark sat back with a sigh of relief. Nobody had died, and it certainly seemed like Ms. Sanchez hadn't been hurt. "Wow," he said. "That's amazing."

"I know," Chloe said, smiling with satisfaction. "I got all of that out of her in just one ten-minute interview!" For the moment, Chloe's pride made her forget about her longing for Clark. "Today, the *Torch* in Smallville High School; tomorrow, the *Daily Planet* in Metropolis." She pressed the keys on her computer to save her article. "Just you watch."

❦ ❦ ❦ ❦

It had been days since Lana had come to the hayloft to read Whitney's letter, and she and

Clark still hadn't talked. Well, they'd spoken: an occasional "hi" in the hallway at school, and Lana had come by Clark's locker to ask how he was doing. But they were alone only for a second before Pete and Chloe joined them, and then Lana said she had to go. "Was it something we said?" Chloe asked. Clark didn't want to get into the whole story with them, so he just made an excuse for Lana's quick exit, something about having to get to her manager's job at the Talon.

Clark hated this uncomfortable feeling between them, and he missed talking to Lana. So this afternoon he was going to go to the Talon, ask Lana to take a break, and apologize to her. Then, hopefully, they could be friends again. Plus, he had a perfect excuse for going there — his mother's organic apple pies were the top-selling dessert at the Talon, and today was delivery day.

Clark pulled his truck to the corner. The *Talon*'s marquee read POETRY SLAM SATURDAY NIGHT. The outside of the building still looked like an old movie theater, but inside, Lana (with Lex's financial help) had restored the crumbling theater and turned it into a very cool place to hang out. Big chairs and couches were everywhere, there was dark-red carpet on the floor, and the soft lighting made it feel cozy. People were lounging around with lattes, talking, and typing on laptops.

Lana was behind the counter running the cappuccino maker when Clark got there.

"Delivery," he said brightly, putting the box of pies on the counter.

Lana turned and smiled haltingly. "Hey," she said. "I thought your mom said she'd be driving these over today." She took the pies from the crate and set them aside.

"I thought I'd save her the trip," Clark said. "That's okay, isn't it?"

Lana grinned. "Of course it's okay," she said. "I feel like I haven't talked to you in ages."

"Me too," Clark said, sliding onto a chair at the counter. "Listen, Lana . . . I'm really sorry about how I acted the other day."

Lana was shaking her head. "You don't need to apologize for anything, Clark. I was dragging you into my personal business, and I shouldn't have."

"But that's not —," Clark faltered, not sure how to continue. He felt that familiar pull of emotion that bound him to Lana, and it gave him courage. *I'm going to do it*, he thought. *I'm just going to tell her how I feel. I've got nothing to lose and everything to gain.* "The thing is," Clark said, "I want you to know —"

At that moment, Clark felt a heavy hand on his shoulder. "Hey, Clark," said a familiar voice. Clark turned around to see a tall blond man in a uniform standing behind him.

"Whitney," Clark said, shocked.

CHAPTER 4

"Dude, how are you?" Whitney smiled, shaking Clark's hand and wrapping his other arm around Clark's shoulders. Clark was too surprised to do anything but shake Whitney's hand, sort of pat him on the back, and exclaim, "Whitney!" again in disbelief. "What are you doing here?"

"Got a weekend pass," he said, grinning. "My whole barracks did because it turns out we're the best marksmen this month." Clark was dazed. *What incredible timing*, he thought. *Just as I'm about to tell Lana I'm in love with her.*

"Besides," Whitney continued, "I miss every-thing — my mom, my friends" — he turned to look meaningfully at Lana — "and one person in particular."

Lana's smile looked pained, Clark thought, but probably not as pained as his own. She looked toward the entrance of the Talon, where a group of people had just come in and taken a table. "Darn," she said. "Duty calls." She left Clark and Whitney, who sat down in the chair next to Clark.

Clark tried to compose himself. "So, how's it going, Whitney?"

"It's going great," he said. "I love the Marines. It's tough, don't get me wrong — I thought basic training was going to kill me." He laughed. "But I finally feel . . . I don't want to get heavy on you, Clark, but I finally feel like I'm doing work that means something. Like maybe *I* mean something."

As Clark listened, he realized that Whitney really had changed. It wasn't just his starched uniform or his crew cut or his ramrod-straight posture, all of which made Whitney look more like a man and less like the high-school senior Clark had known. There was a different look in his eyes.

"I used to think that being the captain of the football team made me special," Whitney said.

"But now I know that that was — well, it was fun, but it didn't mean I was a man. But that's enough from me." Whitney smiled. "How's it going with you, Clark?"

Clark so wanted to tell Whitney about saving Lana from the huge tornadoes that had hit Smallville the day Whitney left for basic training, to tell him about the amazing things he could do that would compare in importance to what Whitney was saying. But he didn't dare; this wasn't a contest he could win without exposing his secret.

"Fine." Clark shrugged. "You know, just normal life in Smallville."

Whitney looked over his shoulder at Lana, who was still taking coffee orders.

"And Lana . . . ," he said. "Is she okay?"

"Yeah," Clark said. "She's fine."

"I really appreciate you looking out for her," Whitney said. "I know that was a lot for me to ask of you, Clark, but you're the only guy I'd really trust."

Clark took in a deep breath. This was all too much. First Lana reading the letter, then Clark coming to tell her the truth about his feelings on the very day that Whitney returns to Smallville. *Just my incredible luck,* Clark thought. And now, if Whitney started talking to him about Lana, Clark thought he might lose it completely.

"It's just that things have been a little tense with Lana," Whitney said. "I think she might be having . . . reservations."

"Yeah." Clark sighed.

Whitney was silent for a second, and then he put a hand on Clark's shoulder — but not in the same way he had when he'd first greeted Clark.

"Wait a minute," Whitney said, his face stony. "What do you mean, 'yeah'? Kent, do you know something I don't?"

"No!" Clark said quickly. "No, I just — Lana mentioned — I mean, I just guessed . . ."

Whitney looked hurt and angry. "Did Lana tell you something about us? About her feelings for me?"

"Boy, can't anybody just order a simple coffee anymore?" Lana said jokingly, returning to the counter. She was greeted by Whitney's shocked expression and Clark's helpless one.

"What's going on?" she asked warily.

"Kent was just leaving," Whitney said pointedly, "so that you and I can be alone for a while."

❧ ❧ ❧ ❧

Clark walked out of the Talon with a heavy heart. He'd gone in there to apologize to Lana and even to tell her how he really felt about her, and instead all he'd done was get her in trouble with Whitney. Even worse, now Lana was probably going to be mad at him for breaking her confidence by talking with Whitney about her feelings, even though he'd hardly said a word. He put the empty pie crate in the back of his truck and wondered how everything could have gone so totally wrong in the space of just five minutes.

"You look like a man who's not having the best day in the world," said a voice behind him.

"Hey, Lex," Clark said, managing a weak smile as he turned to greet his friend.

With his baldness, his expensive dark suit, and his shiny silver Porsche, Lex Luthor was an imposing figure for a twenty-four-year-old guy. He was stopping by, Clark guessed, to collect the week's accounting papers from Lana. He'd bought the Talon from Lana's aunt Nell, at Lana's insistence, to keep it from being turned into a parking lot.

The Talon was a pet project of Lex's; as the son of Lionel Luthor and the sole heir to LuthorCorp, a multibillion-dollar business, Lex probably had a ton of other, more important, business deals to worry about. But Lex admired Lana's hard work on the Talon, and he wanted to encourage her. Besides, helping to save one of Smallville's landmarks might take some of the tarnish off the Luthor family name.

The Luthors had a bad reputation in Smallville. Lex and his father were the rich people who owned the bank, the fertilizer plant, and lots of other businesses in town, and whose dealings were thought to be sketchy at best. Lionel's were, anyway. It was almost two years ago that Lionel had sent Lex to manage the fertilizer plant so that he could learn the family business, and Lex had spent a lot of his time and energy trying to convince the people of Smallville that he wasn't the bad guy everyone thought he was, or at least that he wasn't the heartless villain that his father was.

Even though Clark thought of Lex as a close friend, Lex was barely welcome in the Kent home. Clark's father shared the town's general mistrust of the Luthors and usually excused himself whenever Lex came around. But Clark was glad to see Lex, especially at that moment.

"Do you know what shoes taste like, Lex?" Clark asked. "'Cause I sure do. I just put my foot in my mouth in a major way."

"Let me guess," Lex said smoothly. "Something to do with Lana and the jock." Lex rarely referred to Whitney by name. He knew about Clark's crush on Lana and had always encouraged Clark to go for it, despite her having a boyfriend. Lex didn't seem to share his father's taste for ruthlessness in business, but he definitely possessed the Luthor gene of "win, no matter what."

Clark nodded. "Lana confided something in me, and I think I just spilled the beans to Whitney." He tried to smile.

"I wouldn't worry too much about it. It's probably just going to force a conversation they need to have anyway. There's never any use in hiding things, Clark," Lex said, striding into the Talon. "The truth always comes out."

❦ ❦ ❦ ❦

As he drove home, Clark considered what Lex had said. He was probably right; the truth always did come out, eventually. And one day, Whitney or no Whitney, Clark would be honest with Lana about his feelings for her.

But, Clark thought, he would never be able to be honest with Lex about a very different matter.

Clark remembered the day nearly two years ago when he'd first met Lex Luthor. Lex had been driving down a road when he lost control of his car near a bridge. He'd gone crashing through the bridge railing at sixty miles an hour, straight down into the river below.

Clark had been standing on that bridge. One minute he'd been looking down at the water, deep in thought, and the next he'd heard screeching tires and saw Lex's car heading straight at him. Clark remembered the car slamming into him —

a shock — then the sensation of flying through the air. The last thing he had seen, before the car crashed through the side of the bridge and sent him into the cold water below, was Lex's horrified face.

There had been no time to think. Clark had torn the roof off the car to reach in and save Lex, who was unconscious and drowning. Clark hadn't realized until later, after the ambulance had taken Lex away and Jonathan Kent had whisked Clark home, that he was completely unhurt. Not even a bruise or a scratch.

But Lex had realized it too. It nagged at him, never really leaving his mind. And as much as Clark had tried to convince Lex that the car had just missed him and that he'd jumped into the water to save him, Lex knew — he *knew* — that he'd hit the teenager full force. And there was no explanation for the roof of the car, which had been peeled back like the lid of a can.

Despite their disagreement on what had really happened that day, Clark and Lex had become friends. They had an admiration for each other, and Clark sometimes thought of Lex as a big brother. Occasionally, though, something strange would happen that re-ignited Lex's obsession.

Though Clark never doubted Lex's friendship, he wondered, as he pulled into the driveway of his house, if that obsession would ever really go away.

ை ை ை ை

That night, Clark risked a phone call to Lana. He had to talk to her; he couldn't wait until he saw her at school on Monday to find out what had happened with Whitney, and he didn't dare go to her house with Whitney around.

"Hello?" Lana answered.

"Hey, it's me," Clark said. "Can you talk?"

"Not really. I mean, I can for a second. Whitney and some of his friends are on their way over."

Clark hesitated, unsure how to begin. "I just wanted to apologize," he said. "Did I get you in trouble?"

"Well," Lana said, "we haven't really talked about it yet — I got slammed at the Talon. But it's probably for the best. There are a lot of things that Whitney and I need to talk about, and that kind of opened the door. And you know what they say — what doesn't kill us will make us stronger." Lana was trying to keep her voice light. Clark was silent; he didn't know what to say.

"I have to go," Lana said finally. "Whitney's here."

"Okay," Clark said, not hanging up until he'd heard the click on the other end.

Well, he thought, *either Lana and Whitney are going to break up, or Lana is going to come to school on Monday with an engagement ring on her finger.*

Clark sighed and leaned back on his bed. About the only good thing that had happened this week was that Ms. Sanchez had come to Smallville. Just thinking about her brought a smile back to Clark's face. There was at least one reason to look forward to school on Monday.

CHAPTER 5

Among Clark's chores on Saturday afternoons was putting together crates of vegetables from his parents' farm to be delivered to various stores around town. The crates weighed over a hundred pounds each; Clark lifted them as though they were empty cardboard boxes.

"Hey, Mom," he said, seeing Martha at the doorway. "Almost done here."

"I can see that." She smiled. "By the way, Lana called."

Clark shrugged. "Where do you want these?"

Martha frowned quizzically. "Right over there," she said. "Phone calls from Lana used to generate a little more excitement around here." Clark just shrugged again. "Did you two have words?" Martha asked.

"Kind of," Clark said, "and they were all about Whitney." He sighed. "I just don't think I want to hear anymore about that situation, whatever it is."

"I see," said his mom.

"Besides," Clark said, effortlessly tossing the last huge crate on top of the others, "I've been thinking, and you know what I realized? Lana Lang is not the only girl in Smallville."

"Oh?" Martha said. "And who is this other girl?"

Clark smiled to himself. "That," he said, kissing his mom on the cheek, "is a secret."

❧ ❧ ❧ ❧

That night a quarter moon rose like a smile against the dark backdrop of a million stars, and Lana and Whitney found themselves driving aimlessly through the countryside. It should have been a happy occasion. It was the first time they'd been alone since yesterday, when Whitney had gotten home. Since then he'd been bombarded with friends and relatives, all wanting to see him and ask about life in the Marines.

Lana had been at Whitney's side for most of it, smiling like the dutiful, faithful girlfriend. At last, everyone had backed off so that Whitney and Lana could enjoy some private time alone together.

Now they were together, but they both felt alone.

The ride had been quiet except for the lightest of conversation, like Whitney asking, "Do you want the radio on?" and Lana saying, "Whatever you want." Finally, Whitney stopped the truck on a beautiful hill, the site of their last picnic together before he'd shipped out. She had been afraid that he was going to propose on that day, but what he'd dug out of his knapsack instead of a ring was his induction papers.

Lana had no such fear that Whitney would propose now. She tried to find a way to break this awful silence between them.

"It's beautiful out here," she said. Whitney looked up at the stars and sighed.

"Lana, what's going on?" he asked softly.

She hesitated. "I don't know how to answer that."

Whitney turned to look at her. "With us, Lana. I need to know what's going on with us. Things feel different, and Clark said something yesterday about you having second thoughts."

Lana looked genuinely surprised. "Clark said that?"

"Not in so many words," Whitney said. "I mentioned I was afraid you were, and he kind of agreed. Did you say something to Clark about us? Something you maybe should have said to me?" He didn't seem angry now, just hurt.

Lana wasn't about to lie to Whitney, but she also wasn't about to tell him that she was reading his letters aloud to other people. She searched for the right words. "Clark is my friend, Whitney," she said. "Sometimes I tell him things about myself, things I wonder about."

"Are you . . ." Whitney took in a deep breath. "Are you wondering about us?"

Lana looked away from Whitney and up at the sky, wishing that the answer would come to her from the stars. Why couldn't she be more certain of her feelings? She knew she felt connected to

Whitney in some indefinable way. But then how could she have such intimate conversations about her innermost thoughts and feelings with Clark?

Best not to confuse the issue by bringing Clark into it, Lana thought. Then she told Whitney the truth. "I can only tell you that my feelings about you haven't changed," she began. "It's just that . . . honestly, it's hard for me to explain what my feelings are. But I do know that I have feelings for you."

Whitney nodded calmly. "Okay," he said. "As long as you still have feelings for me, that's enough. I can wait for you to figure them out."

They went back to looking up at the night sky. To Lana, things felt a little more settled, a little more comfortable. Whitney had accepted what she'd said. There was just one thing she still didn't understand.

"Whitney, can I ask you a question?"

"Sure," he said.

"In your letter, you said that the next time we were together, something would happen that would make me realize that we were meant to be together," Lana said. "I don't want to rock the boat again, but . . . what did you mean?"

Whitney smiled warmly at her, a smile Lana knew well. It was the best of Whitney, a smile that came straight from his heart. "Come here," he said, "and I'll show you." He held his arms out to her.

Slowly, Lana went to him and let herself be enfolded. She relaxed against him, letting her head rest on his shoulder. It was like being held by a big, warm blanket.

"See?" Whitney said. "This was what I meant."

Lana's eyes closed, and she felt what she had always felt in Whitney's arms: safe.

CHAPTER 6

Monday wasn't usually any student's favorite day at Smallville High, but Clark was quickly becoming a convert. Spanish was his last class of the day, and he'd spent the whole weekend thinking about Lilia Sanchez and all day looking forward to seeing her. He quickly put his other books in his locker, slammed it shut, and began walking (briskly to anyone else — to him it felt slow) to class. He saw Chloe in the hall but didn't stop to talk. He just threw her a breezy "Hey!" before moving on.

He wasn't the only one who seemed to have a new enthusiasm for Spanish class. For anyone who'd been having trouble with the subject, it had been a torturous embarrassment to fumble for the words in front of everyone. Not that Mr. Hector, their usual teacher, was a drill sergeant, but he could be a bit demanding.

But Ms. Sanchez was much more low-key and encouraging, laughing with people, giving the class a more pleasant vibe. She also seemed to have an uncanny knack for knowing when someone was having a problem, particularly the more nervous students. Ms. Sanchez had guessed that for Patricia Kaye studying at home might be difficult with a large family around; she hadn't been told that Patricia lived in a small house with five younger brothers. Ms. Sanchez had offered to stay for an hour after school for a "homework club"; Patricia could study in peace and quiet, and Ms. Sanchez could grade papers and plan lessons — her own homework, she joked.

And there was Daniel Huang. He'd told Pete that the day Ms. Sanchez had asked him to stay after class, she'd correctly guessed that his parents were immigrants and that they spoke mostly Chinese at home. She put him at ease by telling him about her own parents, who spoke mostly Spanish at home, and about her first year in Smallville and her attempts at speaking English. Then she had suggested that Daniel try to teach his parents the Spanish he was learning at school, which would improve his own understanding of it. He was already more relaxed in class, Clark thought.

Ms. Sanchez had been here only a week, yet she was already getting to know the students better than teachers they'd been with for months. *If only there was some way I could get to know her better,* Clark thought, arriving at the classroom. He felt his heart thudding a little faster than usual in his chest (*And I know that's not because I was rushing,* he thought), and he self-consciously ran a hand over his thick, dark hair before walking into the room.

❧ ❧ ❧ ❧

Ms. Sanchez was writing the day's lesson on the chalkboard. "*Hola, Señor* Kent," she said. Clark couldn't be sure, but it seemed like she'd said that *before* she turned around to see who was there.

"*Buenos días, Profesora,*" he answered. She

grinned at him, then walked over to his desk as he sat down. She leaned over to speak to him, and her nearness was almost intoxicating to Clark. In fact, he even felt a little light-headed, and his stomach jumped. But he couldn't be bothered by it because he was too busy taking in all the details of her: the earthy brown of her eyes framed by long, dark lashes, the slightly cinnamon color of her skin, the silky brown hair he could have happily gotten lost in. He could even smell her fragrance, a fresh, slightly floral scent. Heaven. And then she spoke the words that Clark had been hoping to hear.

"Clark, can I ask you to stay after class for just a moment," she said softly. "I'd like to talk to you about something."

"Sure," was all Clark could say.

❦ ❦ ❦ ❦

If Clark was ever going to win an award for paying attention in class, it wasn't going to be today. Actually, he was paying very close attention to Ms. Sanchez, but he wasn't focusing on the lesson at all. The only thought rolling around in his mind was what she could possibly want to talk to him about.

What did teachers usually ask you to stay after class for? Mentally, he ran through the possibilities. It couldn't be about him having any trouble, like the other kids she'd asked to speak to — he was an A student in Spanish. Had he been talking during class? Nope. A lateness problem? He smiled to himself. *Not likely, when you can run sixty miles an hour.*

Maybe . . . maybe she just wants to talk to me, Clark thought. Maybe she knew he liked her, the way she knew things about other students. Maybe . . .

Clark didn't dare let himself think this way. This was the second girl this week who had asked to talk to him, Lana being the first. The results of that conversation had been a total disaster. *Please don't let it be that Ms. Sanchez wants to talk to me about some other guy,* Clark hoped.

❧ ❧ ❧ ❧

As it happened, Ms. Sanchez did want to talk about another guy, but not in the way that Clark had been worried about.

"You and Pete Ross are good friends, no?" she asked. She went to get her chair from behind her desk, then brought it over and sat down in front of Clark. As she did, Clark's head got a little swimmy again. That was way weird; he'd heard of people *saying* that someone they liked could make them feel faint, but he hadn't thought it could happen literally. Especially to him.

"Yeah," said Clark, hoping his sudden head rush wasn't apparent. "He's one of my best friends."

"I thought so." Ms. Sanchez smiled. "And because you're his friend, you can help me to help him. Pete is having some trouble with verbs. He's nervous about them, I can tell. He's psyching himself out. Do you know what I mean?" Clark nodded, trying to concentrate on what Ms. Sanchez was saying rather than admiring her hair, her neck, her . . . everything.

"I think Pete can come to understand conjugations better," Ms. Sanchez continued, "if someone could speak to him in conversational Spanish. Someone who has a good enough understanding of the language to be able to talk about the things you normally would. And I think that person is you, Clark."

"Me?" Clark said, realizing the compliment she'd given him.

"*Sí*. Your Spanish is very good, good enough to tutor your friend. You are ahead of your grade level right now. But," she said, tempering her words with a smile, "your accent could catch up to your fluency a little. And I think the more you speak Spanish, the better your accent will get."

"So Pete and I will actually be helping each other," Clark said, nodding.

"*Exacto*," said Ms. Sanchez. "So this is all right with you then? I don't want Pete to fall behind, and I thought if you told him the idea, he would be less embarrassed by it."

"Of course I'll do it," said Clark, eager to please her. "Besides, what are friends for?"

"I knew you were the right person to talk to about this," Ms. Sanchez said. And then she did something that would stay with Clark for a long time: she reached over and put her hand on top of his, giving it a little squeeze. It was such a simple gesture, but Clark was amazed at how meaningful it was for him at that moment. He felt the warmth of her hand, the soft pressure of her fingers. And he felt like a thousand tiny birds were in his belly, all beating their wings to get out.

"You are a very special person, Clark," Ms. Sanchez said. "I can sense that about you."

❧ ❧ ❧ ❧

In a daze, Clark walked down the steps of his school. Superspeed was out of the question; he was in superslow motion. *Wow,* he thought. *Wow. Wow. She touched me. She actually leaned over and touched me. And then,* he remembered, enjoying the instant replay of events, *she said I was special.*

He smiled secretively. *If only she knew how special.*

Then, a thought suddenly dropped into Clark's mind like a rock: what if, somehow, Ms. Sanchez *did* know?

He stopped in his tracks. She seemed to know

so much about people without them telling her. Was it possible that she had just correctly guessed all these things? Or was she somehow incredibly intuitive?

Clark began to pace the empty courtyard at school, thoughts rumbling over one another in his mind. No way. Ms. Sanchez couldn't read minds or anything like that . . . could she? She didn't show signs of knowing things about everybody. Clark tried to remember the situations in which she'd been able to guess things about people. She knew about Patricia not being able to study at home; Patricia had almost been in tears when Ms. Sanchez had taken her aside to suggest the study time. Daniel had told Pete before class that he'd been freaking out about his report card, and it was right after that class that Ms. Sanchez had talked to him about how he could bring up his grades. And Pete — she'd let Pete off the hook when the exercise was talking about his family, almost like she knew why he'd been sweating it. She'd known that Clark was at the door before she had even turned around from the blackboard. *And I was a little nervous about seeing her when I got there*, he thought. There seemed to be only one common thread: she knew stuff about people who were anxious, a little hyper. But how? Chloe had just told him the other day about Ms. Sanchez being caught in the meteorite shower. Could that have affected her in some bizarre way?

Abruptly, Clark laughed to himself. *Geez, get a grip*, he thought, shaking his head. A lot of strange things happened in Smallville, but this was a little too way-out. Just because his Spanish teacher was unusually perceptive didn't automatically make her some kind of meteorite-enhanced freak. And besides, she had given Clark no indication that she knew anything about him other than —

Other than that she thinks I'm special, he thought.

It was a very good thing he was alone, he realized, as he walked slowly out of the courtyard, so no one could see the huge goofy smile on his face.

❧ ❧ ❧ ❧

A moment later, Lilia Sanchez headed out of the school. She paused just outside the doorway, rummaging in her purse for her car keys. The darn things always seemed to work their way down to the very bottom somehow. Even if she could find them, she thought, there was only a fifty-fifty chance that her cheap secondhand car would start. Half the time, it just lay there like a lazy dog.

She was so distracted that she didn't hear the creaking noises coming from the scaffolding four stories above.

All week long there had been repair work being done on the bricks at the top of the school's roof. Today was the final day, and the workmen had just finished dismantling one scaffold and were loading it into a truck. On the wooden boards of another scaffold that still hung from the side of the school building, buckets of hardened cement inched slowly to one side as the ropes began to slip from their metal clasps and give way.

Clark turned and saw Ms. Sanchez coming out of school, digging in her purse for something. He felt suddenly awkward — he didn't want her to think he was waiting for her, and he hadn't meant to get so lost in thought that he was just hanging around. *Great, now I look like a total stalker,* he thought, embarrassed. He was about to take off at superspeed when he took one last look at her . . .

And he saw that the scaffolding rigged up on the top of the school building had come loose and was about to come crashing down — right on Ms. Sanchez.

Chapter 7

When he went into superspeed mode, everything around Clark looked like it was almost standing still. As he ran toward Ms. Sanchez in a blur, covering the distance of a hundred yards in a hundredth of a second, he watched as she heard the cracking sound of the scaffolding and looked up; he saw it lurching down toward her, and then he reached her, hurling his body on top of hers. He felt the scaffolding crash on top of him, breaking in half with a loud crack as he dived with Ms. Sanchez in his arms away from the stairs and into the grass. As they fell to the ground, he heard the pieces of the platform hit the steps, the wooden boards shattering into splinters. The heavy buckets hit next with a scary crunch, and bits of cement rained down on them.

Though he knew there was no way he could've been hurt, Clark suddenly felt a little sick. It was the same way he felt whenever he was around meteor rocks, but nowhere near as intense. *What's going on?* he thought. He couldn't see any meteorites, but he could feel them. Squinting slightly, Clark used his X-ray vision. Even that seemed a little fuzzy, but now he could see them well enough: tiny specks of meteorite that had probably been ground and mixed into the cement as filler. Fortunately, they weren't large or numerous enough to do anything but make Clark's stomach feel like it was on a roller coaster.

But even without the meteorites, Clark couldn't blame himself for feeling a little strange. For one thing, Ms. Sanchez had nearly gotten killed. He looked down at her; she was dazed, moaning slightly, her eyes closed. Tiny pieces of the glittering cement were all around them — on her face, in her hair.

For another thing, Clark realized with a flush, he was lying on top of Ms. Sanchez, having tackled her like a football player to get her out of harm's way. But he was too freaked out about whether she was hurt or not to be really worried about that right now.

"Ms. Sanchez?" he said, a small amount of panic in his voice. "Ms. Sanchez, are you okay?" Clark went back into X-ray mode to scan her for any broken bones. He didn't see any, but what he did see stopped him cold: there, embedded in Ms. Sanchez's skull, were tiny bits of meteorite.

How had they gotten there? Was she bleeding? Clark gently stroked the back of her head — no blood. He scanned again. The pieces were so small he could hardly see them, especially since his vision was being affected by the meteorite shards around him, and they were far enough inside her skull that it looked like they must have been there for some time.

Since she was little, he thought. Since the meteor shower. Chloe had told him about the meteorite exploding behind Ms. Sanchez. These tiny fragments could have gotten lodged in her skull back then, so small they couldn't really hurt her.

Or hurt Clark, especially when he was a few

feet away from her, like in class. But the few times he'd been close to her, he *had* felt a little light-headed, a little sick. He'd attributed it to his crush on her, but this explained things a little more.

Clark tried to carefully brush the meteorite-and-cement pieces out of her hair. As he touched them, they burned a little. At least it didn't seem like she'd seen him coming toward her at super-speed. He didn't know how he could have explained that if —

Her eyelids began to flutter. *"If she knew,"* she said dreamily.

"Ms. Sanchez?" Clark said. "What —"

"What if she knew . . . ," Lilia mumbled, *"about my powers? She can't find out, can't tell anyone, can't know my secret . . ."*

❧ ❧ ❧ ❧

A cold sweat broke out all over Clark's body. *Oh, no. This can't be happening. Ms. Sanchez didn't just say what I think she said.*

Now Clark really felt like he was going to be sick. He slowly let go of her and backed away, and as he did he heard the workmen running over to them, shouting with concern. Even being a few feet away from the meteorite flecks made Clark feel better — at least physically.

"Hey kid!" One of the workmen came over to him while two others leaned over Ms. Sanchez. "Are you all right?"

"I'm fine," Clark said. "Nothing hit us." He watched as they helped Ms. Sanchez to her feet. In shock, Clark tried to sort through what had just happened. She *could* read people's minds. The tiny bits of meteorite in her skull must have something to do with it. And she'd just read the mind of the one person in Smallville who probably had the biggest secret to hide.

Cold fear gripped him as he watched Ms. Sanchez dust herself off and look around, her eyes settling on him. What would she say?

"Clark!" Ms. Sanchez exclaimed breathlessly. "You — you pushed me out of the way! Are you hurt?"

"No," Clark said, standing up quickly and going to her side as the workmen brushed the cement off her. "Are you all right?"

"I'm fine, thanks to you," she said, smiling gratefully. "You saved my life, Clark." She reached over and took his hands in hers. "You truly are an amazing person."

Clark felt a little woozy again, but he wasn't entirely sure it was because of the meteorites this time.

🐾 🐾 🐾 🐾

"That's it?" Jonathan Kent asked. "That's all she said?"

Clark sat at the dinner table with his parents. His mother had been happily making her specialty, spaghetti and meatballs, when Clark had come in. As he told the story of what had happened with Ms. Sanchez, dinner had come to a halt, and his parents had identical dropped-jaw looks on their faces.

"That's all she said — to me, at least." Clark

shrugged. "She didn't seem to remember anything. I even sort of hinted at it, like, 'What's the
last thing you remember?' She said she remembered looking for her car keys, and the next thing
she knew, the workmen were helping her up."
Clark paused to take a bowl of spaghetti from his
mother, who had been standing there just holding it for about five minutes as she listened. She
sat down and let Clark dish out the food.

"So you're saying," Martha began slowly, "that
Ms. Sanchez can actually read people's minds?"
She looked at Jonathan, who now looked wor-
ried.

"Well," Clark said, "it sure sounded like she
said what I'd been thinking." He wolfed down an
entire meatball in one bite.

"You don't seem to be too concerned about
this," Jonathan said.

Clark chewed, then answered. "I'll admit I was
pretty freaked out by it at first, but maybe . . .
maybe I was wrong. Or maybe she won't remember it at all."

Or maybe I'm not worried because I'm still thinking

about when she was holding my hand, Clark thought, hoping his parents couldn't suddenly read minds too.

☙ ☙ ☙ ☙

Lex was driving along one of the winding roads that led up to the Luthor mansion when he saw a figure in the distance standing by the road, looking out at a field. As he got closer, he could see she was a petite woman with shiny dark hair. She waved to him, and he pulled up alongside her.

"Can I help you?" Lex said, getting out of his car.

The woman smiled. "Are you Lex Luthor?" she asked.

Whenever someone asked Lex this question, he would tense up slightly. He never knew what people were going to say to him or accuse him of doing. Cautiously, he said, "Yes . . ."

The woman, who was strikingly pretty, Lex noted, extended her hand. "Then I owe you an apology." She smiled. "I'm afraid I'm trespassing. I just needed to take a drive to clear my head, and I ended up here."

Lex shook her hand. *No, not pretty*, he thought. *She's beautiful.* "This seems like a strange place to trespass," he said. "There's not much to look at here."

"Oh, it used to be very pretty," she said. "That mud hole behind us was a pond. And this," — she gestured to the field in front of them — "used to be my father's land."

Lex turned to her with a sheepish look. "Um . . . my father didn't do anything bad to your father to get this land, did he?"

"Oh, no, no," the woman said, laughing. "Nothing like that! My father sold this land willingly. My family was moving back to Madrid."

Whew, Lex thought. "You haven't told me your name," he said.

"*Lo siento*, I'm sorry," she said. "I'm Lilia Sanchez. I'm the new substitute Spanish teacher at the high school."

"Well, Lilia Sanchez, welcome back to Smallville," Lex said. "But I regret to inform you that there is a slight penalty for trespassing around here."

Lilia turned to look at him, not sure what he meant.

"You're going to have to agree to have dinner with me tomorrow night," Lex said.

CHAPTER 8

At the end of Spanish class the next day, Clark put his books away extra slowly. He wanted to hang around for a second to talk with Ms. Sanchez, and he didn't want anyone else to be there. Slowly, the classroom cleared.

"How are you feeling?" Clark asked. "Are you okay after yesterday?"

"*Sí*, I'm fine," Ms. Sanchez said. "I was a little shaken up, I'll admit. But I took a drive to clear my head and felt much better. And actually, while I was out I met a friend of yours."

"Who?" Clark asked.

"Lex Luthor," Ms. Sanchez replied. "He was driving by, and he stopped to talk. He told me he might be willing to help finance a trip to Spain for the entire class." She looked pleased.

"Wow," Clark said. "But that doesn't surprise me. Lex is very generous."

"He seems very kind," Ms. Sanchez said with a faraway look. To Clark, it felt like there was more to it than what she was saying. He tried to imagine Lex, who didn't have a girlfriend, coming upon someone as pretty as Ms. Sanchez, who was about Lex's age. *Well, what would you do if you were him?* Clark tried to shake off the thought, hoping that he wouldn't find out that Lex was into Ms. Sanchez. That would be such a bummer —

"Clark, what you did yesterday was very brave," said Ms. Sanchez, thankfully breaking Clark's concentration. "You saved my life, and I am — well, I'm beyond grateful. I wanted very much to tell people — the newspapers, everybody — about it."

Clark swallowed.

"But," Ms. Sanchez continued, "I thought that you might be the type of person who doesn't like a lot of attention. Am I right?"

Clark nodded. "Not that kind of attention," he said with a weak smile.

"Wait, let me try that again," Pete said. "*La ropa está dura.*"

Clark smiled at his friend. "Okay, that means, 'The clothes are hard.' I think you need to tell me that they're dry. Either that or you need to use more fabric softener." They were in the basement of the Ross house, and Clark had been doing as Ms. Sanchez asked, talking to Pete about everyday things in Spanish. Actually, Pete had been doing pretty well, responding correctly for the most part while he did his chores.

"Dry, dry . . . let me see." Pete thought out loud as he folded his shirts. "Oh! I know: *La ropa está seca.*"

"*Muy bien,*" Clark said. "You're getting better all the time. Now if I could just get my accent to where I didn't sound like a total gringo . . ."

"You worry too much," Pete said. "You're doing great in Spanish. And besides, you're the teacher's pet. Ms. Sanchez loves you."

"Oh, I don't know about that . . . ," Clark said. Pete started chuckling. "What?" Clark laughed, throwing a towel at Pete.

"Come on, Clark, admit it. It's so obvious that you like her." Pete smiled.

"Pete!" Clark frowned unconvincingly. "She's our *teacher*. She's not some cheerleader or something." He couldn't help smiling, though.

"So? She's not what I'd call an old crone, either — the girl just graduated from college, so she's not *that* much older than us, and she's way hot. In fact, if you said you *didn't* like her, I'd say you weren't human." Now Clark had to laugh; Pete had no way of knowing that what he said was pretty ironic.

"Awww, I knew it," Pete said, slapping his friend on the back. "You're busted. You're totally into her."

"Maybe a little," Clark said, hoping he wasn't blushing. "But I'm not the only one."

"What, you've got competition already?" Pete asked. "Who?"

"Lex," Clark said. "They met by accident the

other day. I think he might have asked her out. She was talking to me about him today."

Pete frowned, as he did whenever Lex's name was mentioned. "Clark, man, I can't believe you'd let Ms. Sanchez go out with Lex Luthor. He's a bad dude. I hope you set her straight."

"Pete, Lex isn't a bad guy," Clark said. "He's just got a bad reputation because of his father."

But Pete was having none of it, and his face was stern. "Look, Clark, I know Lex is your friend and all — I don't know *why* he's your friend, but whatever — I just don't like him. You know what the Luthors did to my family."

Clark did know. He and Pete were little kids when Lex's father bought the Rosses' creamed corn factory and turned it into a fertilizer plant, shutting the Rosses out completely. It was just another business deal for Lionel, yet another thing Lex had to live down. Sometimes, Clark felt caught between his two friends, as he was now.

"You know what your problem is, Clark?" Pete asked.

Clark looked at him, wondering where this was going.

"You're one of those way-nice guys," Pete said, breaking into a smile and slapping him on the back. "You just want to be friends with everybody, and you don't want any trouble."

"You got that right," Clark said.

ᘜ ᘜ ᘜ ᘜ

Clark was driving home from Pete's house when he saw Lex jogging next to the road. He honked the horn and pulled over.

"Hey, Lex." Clark smiled. "Don't tell me your gym membership expired." It was a joke; the gym facilities at the Luthor mansion would have made an Olympic team drool with envy.

Lex laughed. "Actually, my landscaper's been after me to take a look at something," he said, slowing to a walk as Clark stopped his truck. "I figured I might as well take a run while I was at it."

To one side of the road, there was a beautiful green field; to the other, what looked like a big crater in the ground. It was about twelve feet deep in the middle, with gentle slopes on either side. There were some big trees rooted at the edges, some of them leaning over diagonally. It looked like a giant had stepped there and left a big muddy footprint.

"Is this it?" asked Clark.

"Doesn't look like much, does it?" said Lex. "Somebody told me it used to be a nice pond with fish in it, but the meteorites came and blitzed the fish into fossils and the pond into, well, this. My landscaper wants me to fill it in or do something with it." He looked into the mud hole. "Right now I'm thinking *pond*," Lex said.

The two began to walk slowly around the mud hole. A few moments passed quietly while Clark searched for a way to bring something up without sounding weird about it. Finally, he said, "So . . . you met my Spanish teacher."

Lex smiled. "Word gets around quickly, doesn't it?"

"Kind of . . . so, are you, uh, going out with her or something?" Clark asked.

"Well, I invited her over for dinner," Lex said. "But I think 'going out' means something a little different in high school." Clark felt his cheeks flush. It seemed like a slightly condescending thing to say, though he was sure Lex didn't mean anything by it.

"So, are you going to tell me?" Lex asked. Clark looked blank. "What Lilia said," Lex clarified. "Did she ask about me?"

"Oh, yeah," Clark said, nodding. "She wanted to know if all the horror stories were true."

Lex suddenly looked alarmed. If Clark Kent had been anyone else in town, he might have enjoyed seeing Lex on the defensive this way. But Clark wasn't the type to torture a friend, and all it took was a sly grin — their shorthand for *Gotcha, I'm totally kidding* — for Lex to relax.

"Good one, Clark," he said, resuming his confident manner. "You had me there for a minute. Okay, so what did Lilia say about me?"

Lilia. Clark didn't like the sound of Lex using Ms. Sanchez's first name, especially when he himself was confined to addressing her as *Profesora* Sanchez. "She just asked if I knew you."

"Oh," Lex said. Then, from out of nowhere: "And did you tell her how we met?"

"No," Clark said. Why did Lex have to bring up that day at the bridge all the time? "Where are you taking her to dinner?" Clark asked, trying to change the subject.

"Dinner's at my place," Lex said. "Why go for pizza when there's a French chef in residence at the Luthor mansion? And besides, dinner in the main dining room, with the candles and the chandelier — it's not too shabby."

Clark looked at Lex, who was smiling to himself. "Well, just remember," Clark said, "Ms. Sanchez — I mean Lilia — isn't like the women you usually go out with. She's different."

Lex abruptly stopped walking. "What do you mean, 'the women I usually go out with'?"

"Nothing," Clark said. "It's just that . . . well, I know you don't exactly have a history of serious relationships. I just wouldn't want Ms. Sanchez to get hurt, that's all."

Now it was Lex who looked hurt, and surprised. Clark sensed he'd crossed a line, but it was too late to take it back. A not-too-friendly smile spread slowly across Lex's face.

"Ohhhh, now I get it," Lex said. "Somebody's

hot for his teacher, is that it?" He laughed. "Well, I hate to break it to you, my friend, but *Ms. Sanchez* is a little out of your league. Why don't you stick to following Lana Lang around like a puppy dog? I think that's a little more your speed."

Clark had experienced rage only a few times in his life, usually when someone was threatening his parents. What he was feeling now was a very different sensation — the heat of anger mixed with humiliation. He wasn't thinking as he took a super-fast lunge toward Lex, his hands reaching out to grab him.

CHAPTER 9

Lex felt something — a sudden breeze? — and saw only a blur. But in that split second, unknown to Lex, Clark was waging one of the biggest battles of his young life.

Clark had always known he was different from other people. When he was little, his parents had done their best to make sure their adopted son didn't do anything that would call attention to him, make people start asking questions. Then, when he'd gotten old enough to understand, he kept his special abilities hidden as well as he could.

Most of the time, Clark wished that he could be like everyone else, that he could just fit in. If he were normal, he wouldn't have to be so secretive, wouldn't have to monitor his powers all the time.

But there were also times that Clark loved having superpowers. It was just so cool to be able to slam a fence post the size of a tree trunk into the ground by hammering it once with his fist; to smash a boulder that would've taken a normal person and a truck to move into tiny pieces of gravel; to lift a two-ton tractor, as he had the other day, while his Dad smiled gratefully.

But there was a danger, a potential dark side that his parents had repeatedly warned Clark about. Acting without thinking, they had said, could have disastrous results. Clark's father had even forbidden him to join any of the sports teams at Smallville High, afraid that Clark might forget himself, lose control, and hurt somebody.

All it would take is just one second, his father had said. *I know you wouldn't mean to, but you could kill someone.*

In that instant by the mud hole, all Lex could see was a blur before him. But Clark could see himself in slow motion, charging at Lex with anger in his heart and two super-strong hands reaching for his friend.

Suddenly, Clark stopped himself. *No.* Any other guy would have been able to give a friend who was being a jerk the kind of shove that just meant *back off* but that caused no physical damage. If Clark did that, as he wanted to now, he would likely push Lex all the way into next week. He couldn't — wouldn't — ever hurt anyone, if he could possibly help it. Especially a friend, like Lex.

It had only been a fraction of a second and a distance of six feet or so, but Clark was so horrified by what he'd almost done that he didn't realize he'd come to a halt with his hands clutching Lex's sweatshirt.

To Lex, it seemed like his friend had just taken a giant, incredibly fast step and was suddenly upon him. Startled, his reflexes kicked in: he pushed Clark away with all his might.

If they had been on level ground, Lex's push wouldn't have even been enough to move Clark an inch. But they were at the edge of the mud hole, and Clark — taken by surprise — lost his footing. Before he knew what was happening, he was rolling down the slippery slope.

"Clark!" Lex shouted.

The fall itself was nothing. Even a little kid would've dusted himself off and laughed. But as Clark slid toward the bottom of the mud hole, what felt like a bolt of lightning shot through his body. He cried out in sudden agony.

Clark had come to rest a couple of yards away from a large rock about half his size. Even under its coating of dirt, Clark could see it begin to glow green — a meteorite, the biggest one he'd ever seen. Even tiny meteorites, like the one on Lana's necklace, could bring on a pain so great that Clark would wish for unconsciousness to come just to end it. But this one . . .

Clark felt like he was being pierced by a thousand searing needles, like every one of his cells was being ripped apart.

Like he was dying.

❧ ❧ ❧ ❧

"Clark!" Lex shouted. "Clark, are you okay?" Hanging on to a small tree at the edge of the slope, Lex began to climb down into the crater. Dirt and small pebbles gave way under his sneakers, and he had to grab onto scrub weeds to keep himself from sliding down to the bottom too.

As his halting steps brought him closer to Clark, Lex could hear his friend gasping. Alarm rose in his chest as he saw Clark writhing in pain. Lex had never seen Clark like this — had he hurt his spine? Broken a rib and pierced a lung? Sweat broke out all over Lex's body, and he heard his father's voice intoning darkly in his head: *You're in trouble now, aren't you, son?*

The hell with my father, Lex thought. "Clark! Grab my hand!" he shouted, wondering how he was going to pull Clark, who was bigger than him, out of the mud hole. *I'm no super hero,* he thought bitterly. *But I've got to try.*

Clark felt like every one of his veins was threatening to burst. He could even see them throbbing through his skin. But somehow, Lex's voice cut through the pain, and with the last bit of strength Clark had, he lifted his arm toward Lex, reaching for his outstretched hand.

Lex grabbed Clark's wrist and pulled as hard as he could. He looked back at the hunk of scrub weed he was hanging on to. *You'd better have some deep roots*, he mentally told the weed, *or I'll turn this whole place into a parking lot.* Miraculously, it held.

Even the couple of inches Lex was able to pull Clark away from the meteor rock lessened the pain enough for Clark to dig his work boots into the side of the slope and climb up as Lex pulled. Both of them tried to maintain a foothold in the dirt and mud as they climbed farther up.

Clark felt life coming back into his body with every inch of distance he put between himself and that green meteorite. He was almost to the top of the slope, then pulling himself over it, but Lex didn't relax his grip on Clark's arm until they were both over the side and on level ground, panting in the dirt.

At that point, Clark felt fine; he was far enough away from the rock to feel as if nothing had happened, even though he was sure he'd never forget the intensity of the pain he'd just experienced.

He glanced over his shoulder into the pit. That wasn't just a meteorite. It was practically a boulder.

Using his X-ray vision, Clark scanned the mud hole. He could see about a dozen meteorites under the dirt. They were all much smaller than the big one, but still there. *I'm not sure if anything else on this earth can hurt me*, he thought, *but those things can kill me*. He made a mental note to stay well clear of this place.

Lex, still alarmed, leaned over to Clark. "Are you all right? What happened? Do you need an ambulance? I can call —"

"I'm fine, I'm fine." Clark waved Lex away. "Really, I'm okay."

"*Okay?* You looked like you were dying down there! What happened?" Lex asked.

Clark realized that Lex had seen him in the agony the meteorites brought on. He had to think quickly. "I . . . think I had a muscle spasm," he said. Then, more convincingly, he tried to stand up. "Ow!"

"That was more than a muscle spasm. I'm taking you to the hospital," Lex said firmly.

"No!" Clark said, grabbing Lex's arm. "I — I hate hospitals. Really, I think I just pulled a muscle in my back or something. Maybe you could just drive me home."

Lex looked dubious. Clark held his breath, waiting to see whether Lex would challenge him again, knowing that Lex probably didn't believe him.

But Lex just loaded his friend carefully into Clark's truck, and they drove toward the Kent Farm in silence.

CHAPTER 10

"**W**hat happened?" said Martha Kent, concern creasing her face. At the door to the kitchen stood her son, whose hand was on his back as though he was in pain, and Lex Luthor, who appeared to be holding Clark up.

"It's nothing," Clark said, walking into the living room with Lex still supporting him. "I just fell." Lex carefully helped Clark to the couch.

"Fell? What —" Jonathan Kent was utterly confused as he knelt by Clark. "Son, are you hurt?"

Lex finally spoke, wishing he didn't have to. "He says it's just a muscle spasm, but I think he should go to the hospital." Jonathan Kent's eyes fell sharply on Lex, making him feel like a little boy. "Just to be sure," Lex said quietly.

"Really, I'm fine," Clark said. "Nothing a couple of hours on the couch and some pizza won't cure. You know me," he said, trying to defuse his father's anger, "always looking for a way to get out of baling hay."

Clark had hoped at least his mother would laugh at his weak joke, but the tense scene in front of him stayed fixed: his mother's worried face, his father's accusing glare, Lex looking like he wished he could fall back into the mud hole.

Finally, Mom to the rescue. "Lex, we'll take care of it from here," she said, crossing the room to usher him out gently. "Thank you for bringing Clark home." Through the screen door, Clark could see Lex looking guiltily at Jonathan, even though he'd done nothing wrong. He heard Lex walk for a few steps, then begin to jog away.

"He's gone," Martha said. "Are you really hurt?"

"No," Clark said, standing up from the couch. "I'm fine. I just couldn't let Lex know that I was fine."

"Son, what happened?" Jonathan asked.

Reluctantly, Clark told them. With every minute he could see his father's anger rise. Clark tried to downplay the incident, but when he was done, his father slapped the wall.

"Fell?" Jonathan shouted. "Are you sure he didn't *push* you down that slope?"

"Jonathan," Martha said cautiously, more because of the look on Clark's face than because she doubted what her husband was implying.

"Dad, Lex wouldn't do that —," Clark said.

"How do we know what he's capable of doing?" his father thundered. "He's a Luthor, after all —"

"Dad —"

"For heaven's sake, he drove his car right into you —"

"Dad!" Clark rarely raised his voice to his parents, and his father looked surprised. "Lex didn't push me down that slope. He was —" Clark hesitated. "He was pushing me *away*."

Jonathan and Martha looked at Clark, trying to comprehend what their son was saying. "I got mad," Clark explained. "I . . . I kind of lost it."

The look on his parents' faces pained Clark almost as badly as the meteorites did. "I didn't hurt him!" he said quickly. "I stopped myself! I just . . . I kind of lost control for a second."

The moment the words left his mouth, Clark wished he could have taken them back. Those were almost exactly his father's words of warning: *All it would take is just one second . . .*

His parents looked at each other, and Clark watched a million messages fly between them. For all his amazing powers, he couldn't decipher this secret language of the eyes that his parents had, though he knew right now it had everything to do with him.

His father broke the silence. "I'd . . . better get to the supply store before they close," he mumbled. Clark winced inwardly; it was a trip his father usually asked him to come along for.

As if making up for it, Martha quickly said, "Clark, why don't you stay here and do your chores," though Jonathan had already walked out the door.

❧ ❧ ❧ ❧

Martha Kent found her son in the barn, silently stacking bales of hay. She noticed he was doing it slowly, methodically; it was a task that, with his strength and speed, Clark could normally finish in seconds. She cleared her throat, though she knew he'd heard her come in.

"Why is Dad mad at me?" he said, his voice full of hurt.

"Sweetie, he's not mad at you," Martha said. "It's just —"

"It's just that he's tired of having a freak for a son?" Clark let a hay bale drop heavily.

"Clark," Martha said. "Come here. Sit down." They sat together on the hay bale, Martha putting her arm protectively around Clark's shoulders.

"All your life, ever since we found out you were . . . special," Martha said, choosing her words carefully, "your father and I have tried to make sure that there were never any accidents involving your gifts. But you know what?" Clark looked up. "We never really had to worry. You're a good person, Clark. We know you'd never hurt anyone."

"Then why is Dad so angry?" Clark asked. "Why did he leave like that?"

Martha sighed. "He's afraid," she said. "Afraid

that someday, something is going to happen that will force you to use your special abilities, and that someone will see you and . . ." Martha trailed off.

It was a scenario the Kent family rarely spoke about out loud, but it hung in the air, always at the back of their minds. Someone would see Clark do something amazing and inexplicable. Questions would come — how could a teenage boy have such incredible strength, or be able to survive an explosion without being hurt, or have a bullet bounce off his skin? — and then, inevitably, men from the government. They would find the spaceship that was hidden in the storm cellar, and they would take Clark away.

When Clark was about ten, his parents had rented the movie *E.T.: The Extra-terrestrial*. They'd all enjoyed the movie up to the point where the bad guys — people from the government — took E.T. away to study him. Everyone got kind of quiet at that part. Clark asked why they'd taken E.T.; his mother carefully said it was because he was different. Clark hadn't known about the spaceship hidden in the storm cellar back then, but he did know that he was different from any other kids he knew.

That night, Clark had dreamed that he was snatched away from his parents and taken to a giant white room by men in lab coats who tried to dissect him. The dream had been vivid. Even now, Clark shuddered at the memory.

Martha hugged her son. "Don't worry, sweetie. Nothing's going to happen. And your father's not mad at you. He's just scared that he won't be able to protect you."

"It's funny," Clark said. "All the things that can't hurt me, and Dad still worries about protecting me."

Martha laughed. "That's something that will never change, even when you go to college, even when you grow up, even if you move to Metropolis." She was happy to see her son smiling again. "Now," she said, "what was that about you and Lex fighting over your Spanish teacher?"

"Aw, Mom . . ." Clark felt himself blush.

CHAPTER 11

When Lex finally reached the Luthor mansion, he wasn't looking or feeling too well. He was covered in mud and sweat, and he was exhausted. And the long run home hadn't helped him forget about what had happened with Clark.

The whole afternoon had been bad; he didn't like arguing with his friend, and somehow Clark had ended up getting hurt, even though he denied that he was. And the way Jonathan Kent had looked at him made Lex want to cover himself in even more dirt until he was buried completely.

Now Lex had only an hour to get cleaned up and dressed before Lilia, Clark's pretty teacher, showed up, and he was in no mood for entertaining.

Waiting for him inside was more bad news. The butler handed Lex a message. Lex's father had called, threatening to "drop by" within the next few days to go over Lex's accounting. The translation was simple: Lionel Luthor was going to try to take something important away from Lex, like control of the factory. And knowing Lionel, he wouldn't pass up an opportunity to humiliate Lex in front of other people in the process. He thought it made his son stronger.

Damn it, Lex thought. *And damn him.*

Disgusted, Lex crumpled the message and threw it to the floor.

ప ప ప ప

By the time the huge clock in the marble hallway had chimed eight times and Lilia Sanchez had arrived (in the limousine Lex had sent to get her), Lex at least looked composed, if still a bit rattled from the afternoon.

But the sight of Lilia immediately made him feel better. She wore a simple but pretty black dress and an open, friendly smile. People usually didn't smile like that at Lex. They smiled fearfully or greedily, but not warmly, as this woman did.

He had wanted to impress her, to show off a little, by having dinner in the main dining room, which looked like something out of King Arthur's knights of the Round Table. But after a few minutes of seeing how unpretentious and down-to-earth Lilia was, Lex whispered to his butler that dinner should be served on the balcony instead, where a small, intimate table was set with candles.

Lex had been with enough women to be able to see very clearly the games they played with him. He knew that most, if not all, of them had been far more attracted to his money than to his looks or personality. It had kept him from being able to trust almost anyone.

Yet with Lilia, Lex felt his guard coming down. True, he thought at first that she wanted something from him — he had persuaded her to have dinner with him to talk about financing a trip to Spain for Lilia's students. But she brought that topic up in a lighthearted way.

"It would be great for the kids," said Lilia.

"And for you," Lex replied.

Lilia dismissed his comment with a wave of her hand. "I'm only a substitute until Mr. Hector gets back; you should set up the trip no matter who accompanies the students."

"That's a very selfless gesture on your part," Lex said.

Lilia smiled gently. "You must be very used to people wanting something from you."

Lex shrugged. "Most people can be pretty greedy, given half an opportunity."

"Oh, I don't know," Lilia said. "I think people are basically good at heart. It's just circumstances that make them act badly. Don't you think?"

I think you're probably the only truly good person here, Lex thought, suddenly feeling something unfamiliar: a pleasant sort of giddiness. Was he actually nervous? He hadn't felt that nice jittery feeling that came from being around someone he liked in a long time.

"I try to be a good person," Lilia said, staring out at the dark woods. "But I know I can't be truly good always. No one can."

Lex was surprised. It was like she was reading his thoughts. Coincidence, he mused.

"I have a map of Spain in my study," Lex said. "Why don't you show me where you'd like to take the class?"

❧ ❧ ❧ ❧

Lex had spread the map on his desk, and Lilia was happily pointing to one place after another — where certain museums were, the house that the artist Gaudí had built and lived in, Picasso's studio. Her excitement was contagious, and part of Lex wondered for a minute what his father would think of entrusting his multibillion-dollar business to a son who was much happier helping a schoolteacher plan a trip for a bunch of kids than he was managing a huge corporation. Lex stood next to Lilia, close enough to smell her hair. She was achingly lovely.

"And I would want them to see Barcelona," she said. "It's a great city, full of culture . . . ooh, what is that?" Lilia pointed at a rough green rock on Lex's desk.

"That? My landscaper gave it to me this morning," Lex said. "It's a meteorite from that former pond you were standing by yesterday. He figured I could use this as a paperweight." He picked up the stone and held it out to Lilia.

"So this is what they really look like. I never realized they were so pretty," she said, reaching for it.

As Lilia's fingers touched the stone, Lex brushed her hand with his. He'd hoped to hold her hand, to feel the softness of her touch. Instead, he watched, horrified, as her eyes suddenly rolled back in her head.

"*My father . . . ,*" Lilia intoned in a low, guttural voice. "*I hate my father . . . I hate him, hate him; why, why does he have to come here? What does he want from me? Why can't he just love me? Why can't he just love me the way that Clark's parents love him? Why —*"

Lex was stunned. Lilia looked like she was having some kind of seizure, her eyes rolled far back in her head, her body stiff with shock. But she was talking. Her voice was rambling, narrating a stream of consciousness. They weren't her thoughts, though, Lex realized with mounting alarm. They were his.

"Clark," Lilia was saying, *"Clark, why can't I stop wondering about Clark? Why is Clark such a mystery? That day on the bridge, why can't I let it go? Am I jealous of him? He's my friend, but there's something about him I can't figure out. Why can't I just forget it? I won't forget it, never, never, NEVER —"*

My God, Lex thought. *She's reading my mind.*

❦ ❦ ❦ ❦

"Lilia!" Lex shouted, grabbing her by the shoulders and shaking her. The meteorite fell to the floor, and as it did, Lilia stopped speaking.

Slowly, she opened her eyes. "Oh," she said, holding Lex's shoulders. "I . . . what happened?"

"Here," Lex said, pulling a chair close to her. "You'd better sit down. Are you all right? I think you had a seizure — should I call a doctor?"

"No, no," Lilia said, sitting down slowly. "I'm fine; I'm okay. This has happened before. It's not serious — I just kind of black out for a second or two." She smiled. "Really, I'm okay. This makes twice in one day for you, huh?"

Lex knelt down beside her, his heart pounding with nervousness. "What do you mean?"

Lilia looked confused. "Didn't you mention a friend having an accident today? Someone who got hurt?"

"No," Lex said. "I didn't." He was too freaked out to admit that she was right — he'd wanted to take Clark to the hospital after his fall. But he hadn't told her about that.

"I must be thinking of someone else," Lilia said. "Really, I'm fine. I think I should probably just go home."

❧ ❧ ❧ ❧

Thousands of nights in his life, and Clark had never had any trouble sleeping. But on the one night he wished he could just drop off and see the end of a long, rotten day, his eyes refused to close.

Bad enough there had been the whole weird

afternoon with Lex. Then, his father seemed to be mad at him — no matter what Mom said about him just being worried. After Jonathan had come home from the feed store, he had barely spoken all through dinner. And on top of all that, there was the awkwardness with Lana. No wonder he couldn't sleep.

Well, Clark thought, if he was going to be awake, at least he could try to forget all that stuff and think about something nice instead. And Lilia Sanchez was the first thing that came to his mind.

"Mi profesora," Clark said, smiling to himself in the dark. He thought about the way she'd reached over and touched his hand that day at school. Wasn't that something girls did when they liked you?

He couldn't remember feeling this way about anyone besides Lana. But, Clark realized, the feelings he now had for Ms. Sanchez — Lilia — were the same as the ones he had for Lana. He'd been jealous of Lex the same way he'd been jealous of Whitney, and it couldn't just be the microscopic shards of meteorite buried in Lilia's skull that gave Clark such butterflies in his stomach (*More like helicopters,* he thought) whenever he was around her.

But this was different from the painful longing that he felt for Lana, who would probably never be his. It was more like this fantastic anticipation that he felt whenever he thought about Lilia. *Maybe this is what love feels like,* Clark thought.

Clark wondered what it would be like to be alone with her, what it would be like to kiss her, to pull her close to him, and . . .

He fell asleep smiling.

❧ ❧ ❧ ❧

In his dream, Lilia was standing in front of him. She was wearing a white dress. She looked ethereal, angelic; she even seemed to be floating.

Clark . . .

And in the dream, she was reaching toward him, just like she had at school. But not like she had at school; this was different somehow. Wonderful. She was smiling at him, motioning for him to come closer —

Clark . . .

And Clark was reaching out to her, waiting to feel her warm touch, waiting to —

"Clark!"

His Dad's voice — *what*? — what time was it? Clark woke up with a start and turned to look at his alarm clock. It wasn't there — and neither was his night table. *Where* — ? He turned his head a little more. There was the alarm clock, and his night table, and his bed . . . all about four feet below him.

"Clark? What was that? Son, are you all right?"

As quickly as he'd realized he was floating over his bed, Clark had come crashing down on it, falling over the side and onto the floor. This wasn't the first time it had happened, this levitating thing. He'd once had a dream about Lana and had woken up hovering over his bed. But just because it had happened before didn't make it any less freaky, and it took Clark a second, and another shout from his father downstairs, to answer, "I'm fine, be down in a minute!"

Wow. Having special abilities, as his mom liked to call them, sure kept life interesting. One minute you've got a headache and the next minute you can see through things. And now this floating business . . .

Clark found it unsettling until he remembered the dream that had caused it. Suddenly, his mood was a little lighter.

❦ ❦ ❦ ❦

"Are you still willing to be the delivery person for me?" Clark's mom asked. "I've got a million things to do today, and it'd be a big help if you could deliver some vegetables after school."

"Sure thing, Mom," Clark said, reaching into the fridge for the orange juice. "Where am I headed?"

"Just to the organic market, and Anderson's . . . and Lex's house," she said, putting on her jacket. Lex had a standing order for a crate of vegetables from the Kent Farm every week.

Clark was about to take a big gulp from the orange juice container, but set it down instead. "Mom . . . I can't go to Lex's after what happened yesterday. He and I . . . well, things are weird with us right now." Clark looked slightly pained.

"I know, sweetie," Martha said. "But there's no sense in prolonging this. It's best to just go talk to Lex and get whatever this is out in the open. Besides, after the way your father looked at him yesterday, maybe you should go over there and at least let Lex know you're okay."

❧ ❧ ❧ ❧

Clark drove up to the back entrance of the Luthor mansion, hoping maybe that way he wouldn't have to see Lex. He'd put it off, making it the last delivery of the afternoon. But as he was setting the crate of vegetables in the kitchen, he felt guilty. This wasn't the way to deal with a friend. He walked to the library and peered in through the open door.

Clark knocked softly. "Hey."

"Hi," Lex said, looking up from his desk. "Come on in. How's your back?" There was genuine concern in Lex's voice.

"It's fine," Clark said, unsure of what else to say. Lex looked uncomfortable too.

"Listen, Clark," Lex began, "about yesterday . . ."

"I'm sorry," Clark blurted out. "It was all my fault. I was acting like a total jerk, and then I got hurt" — a lie, but one that he had to maintain — "and the whole thing was all my fault."

"Well," Lex said, getting up and walking out from behind the desk, "I wouldn't say you were a *total* jerk. Maybe a partial jerk . . ." Here he grinned, unable to keep a straight face, and Clark grinned back. "Besides," Lex said, "I think I owe you an apology too. I was baiting you, and I said things I shouldn't have."

Clark remembered what Lex had said about him following Lana around like a puppy dog. "Nothing that wasn't true," he said, looking down at the floor.

"Neither true nor kind, my friend," Lex said.

"You're not the only guy in town who can be a jerk." He patted Clark on the back.

Clark relaxed, grateful that the weirdness between him and Lex was over. "She's pretty special, isn't she?" Lex said, striding back to his desk.

"Lana?" Clark asked.

"I was referring to Ms. Sanchez," Lex said. "You must like her an awful lot to go up against a Luthor." He smiled to make sure Clark knew he was kidding.

Clark shoved his hands in his pockets. "I must have been out of my mind to think that . . . ," he began. "I mean, she's my teacher. It's totally ridiculous . . . right?"

In the back of his mind — well, actually, right at the front of his mind, he admitted to himself — Clark was hoping that Lex would say something like, *Ridiculous? Of course it's not ridiculous for you to be in love with your teacher!* And then Lex would tell him some great story about how, when he was at boarding school, he'd fallen in love with his chemistry teacher or something, and how it had actually worked out — that she had fallen in love with him too. Lex would say, *Clark, I've got an idea*, and he'd come up with some genius plan so Clark could win Lilia over, so things could actually work out all right.

Lex could make magic happen. Hadn't he brought the Metropolis Sharks football team to Smallville one night just so Whitney's father could see his son play with the pros before he passed away? Hadn't he set up a fireworks display that must have cost thousands of dollars for Clark's first-ever parents-away blowout party? Hadn't he —

Clark's thoughts were interrupted by the sound of Lex laughing gently. "Yeah, it is kind of ridiculous," he said. "But sweet. I had my share of crushes on older women in school too. But these things don't tend to turn out the way you want them to, Clark."

"Yeah," said Clark, suddenly uncomfortable again. "I guess people can get some pretty crazy thoughts in their heads." He looked at Lex, whose brow was now furrowed pensively. "Something wrong?"

Lex looked up. "Sometimes people can get some pretty crazy thoughts *out* of other people's heads too."

"What do you mean?"

Lex smiled, but he was still thinking something through. *Nothing about me, I hope*, thought Clark.

"Do you believe that people can read minds, Clark?" Lex asked.

CHAPTER 12

Clark was taken aback, but he tried not to show it and smiled at his friend. "Now you're beginning to sound like Chloe hunting down something for her Wall of Weird."

"You didn't answer my question," Lex said. "Do you think it's possible for your thoughts to be read? For your secret, innermost conversations with yourself to be heard by someone else?"

Suddenly wary, Clark wondered what Lex was getting at. They had just put the business of yesterday afternoon behind them, but Clark could tell that the part of Lex that seemed obsessed with finding out the truth about Clark — sometimes even at the expense of their friendship — had just been reawakened.

"I don't know," Clark answered carefully. "I

believe in intuition, but reading thoughts? That sounds a little out there for me."

"Mmm," Lex said as he began to pace slowly in front of his desk. "When Lilia was over last night" — he turned to look at Clark to prove his sincerity — "and I assure you, it was a strictly G-rated evening, she said some . . . interesting things."

Oh, no. Clark tried to look calm. "Interesting, like what?"

"Interesting in that they were things she couldn't possibly have known," Lex said, "unless she had rented a room in my head."

Inwardly, Clark sighed with relief. Lex might have found out about Lilia's special ability, but he didn't seem to be referring to Clark or his secret. "Maybe she overheard something when she came in," he said.

"Maybe," Lex said, standing in front of Clark. "Has anything like that ever happened with you? I mean, with you and Lilia?"

Clark froze — that day at school, when he'd pushed Lilia out of the way of the falling scaffolding. There had been that moment right after the accident when she'd said exactly what Clark was thinking. It was almost like a freaky ventriloquist's joke with a live dummy.

Somehow, the same thing must have happened with Lex when Lilia was with him. And though Clark had no mind-reading abilities that he knew of, he suddenly saw very clearly the thought taking root in Lex's mind.

He thinks Lilia knows something about me.

"No," Clark said. "Nothing like that ever happened."

Lex seemed to look at him for a long time. To Clark, it almost felt like Lex was trying to bore a hole into his brain to see if he was telling the truth. "You know what I think, Clark?" Lex said.

Clark didn't answer.

"I think all the strange things that happen in this town are finally getting to me and that I'm losing it." Lex smiled.

❧ ❧ ❧ ❧

Clark walked down the long marble hallway that led out of the Luthor mansion. He was glad that he and Lex had finally gotten things straightened out, but unnerved at Lex's discovery about Lilia and her unique power. At least, Clark thought, Lex hadn't found out anything from Lilia that had to do with Clark or his abilities. *I hope.*

As he walked down the hall, a butler headed in the opposite direction toward the library. Clark, lost in thought, barely noticed the small black gift box the butler was carrying.

"Hey," said Clark, though the staff of the Luthor mansion rarely spoke back.

True to form, the butler nodded stiffly as he passed Clark. And very suddenly, Clark felt a wave of nausea wash over him. He felt dizzy, just for a second . . . and then it passed, and he was all right again. *What the . . . ?*

He turned to look at the butler, who was already closing the door to Lex's office behind him.

Weird, Clark thought. There didn't seem to be any meteorites around that could make him feel that way, and it was so brief — *Strange,* Clark thought, *but whatever.* He'd been exposed to so much of that bad meteorite power lately, he was wondering if he was starting to imagine feeling sick now.

Realizing that he was running late for dinner, he jogged out of the Luthor mansion to his truck.

☙ ☙ ☙ ☙

If Clark had paused for a second to use his X-ray vision, he would have been able to see past the door to Lex's office as the butler handed the box to Lex. Inside the box was a bracelet Lex had asked a jeweler in town to custom design. It was made of small polished stones bound by a slim silver chain.

Anyone looking at the stones without the benefit of X-ray vision would have thought they were emeralds, they were such a brilliant green.

☙ ☙ ☙ ☙

Lex looked out the stained-glass window of the library, watching Clark drive away. Lex's father had taught him many things — one of them was how to tell whether a person was lying or not.

And when Clark had said that there had never been a time when Lilia Sanchez had voiced his thoughts, Clark had most definitely been lying. Of that, Lex was sure.

What he wasn't sure of was what Lilia would have seen in Clark's mind, or if she would even remember it if she had. She certainly hadn't given Lex any indication that she remembered what she'd said last night. She just thought she'd had a momentary blackout.

It all seemed too unbelievable. Lilia was probably just incredibly intuitive. And all she would have picked up from Clark was his sweet crush on her, and — Lex smiled to himself — he probably wasn't the first.

But no, it seemed to be more than that. Lex had hardly been able to sleep last night, replaying the incident in his head. First, she had correctly guessed that he had trouble trusting people. That hardly took a rocket scientist. But later, when the words — his words, his exact thoughts about his father, and about Clark! — had come tumbling out of her, almost unstoppable —

Lex stared out the window, his fingers absently

stroking the black gift box on his desk. He'd thought she was having a seizure before he realized what she was saying. He'd taken her in his arms to keep her from falling. Even when she had insisted she was all right, he hadn't wanted to let go of her . . .

Concentrate, Lex thought. *You were onto something there. Something about Clark . . .*

Lex tried to keep his train of thought going. What if something similar had happened with Clark and Lilia? What if, somehow, she had been able to see into his mind, to read his thoughts as clearly as she'd read Lex's?

What if she knows something about what really happened the day my car went off that bridge?

If she did, and if Lex could figure out some way to get it out of Lilia, the mystery that haunted him would finally be solved.

And, he thought, he could lose the only close friend he'd ever had, and he could lose the girl as well.

Lex sighed. Anything worth having usually came with a big price tag. But was he prepared to push this envelope with Clark again? After all, no matter how he had done it, Clark had saved Lex's life. Lex owed him big-time for that. But his repeated questions and investigations about that day had put their friendship to the test.

And what about Lilia? Even if Lex could figure out a way to find out if she'd read Clark's thoughts, would it hurt her in some way? Surely those seizures she had while in that trance couldn't be harmless.

Almost immediately, Lex had a gut reaction: *I won't hurt her. I don't care what I could find out.*

He was surprised at himself. His father would have been disgusted. But just thinking about Lilia chased any ideas about forcing some crazy science-fiction experiment with Clark and Lilia straight out of Lex's mind.

Instead, Lex began constructing a very different fantasy. It involved leaving the ruthless business of LuthorCorp, his father, and everything he knew and hated behind, and running away somewhere, anywhere, with Lilia.

From outside, Lex heard the low rumble of thunderclouds in the distance. It sounded like the gods were daring him to defy his father and his destiny.

CHAPTER 13

The next afternoon found Lex waiting until the school bus passed to walk around the corner to the front of Smallville High School. He felt weird about deliberately making sure that Clark had left, but he wasn't eager to run into him and have to explain what he was doing there. In his pocket was the small black gift box his butler had brought him the day before.

After a few minutes, Lex's patience was rewarded. Lilia Sanchez came out of the building (pausing, he noticed, to look up toward the roof for some reason) and headed down the steps. When she saw Lex, she waved and smiled. Lex tried to put the brakes on a huge grin that was about to give him away completely.

"This is a nice surprise," said Lilia. "What brings you here?"

"I wanted to see if you were all right after the other night," he said.

"Yes," she said. "I'm absolutely fine. But you didn't have to come all this way just for that . . ."

"I didn't," Lex said. "I came all this way because I have something for you." Lex held out the elegant black box, which was tied with a red silk ribbon.

Lilia smiled, but hesitated. "Lex . . . ," she said.

He gently pushed it at her again. "Go on." He smiled. "Open it."

Slowly, Lilia opened the box. Inside was the bracelet, its highly polished stones sparkling green.

"Meteorites," Lex said. "You admired the one on my desk, so I thought you might like this."

"Lex . . . ," Lilia said, holding the box out to him. "I can't accept it."

"I don't see why not," Lex said. "It's not like they're diamonds or anything. These rocks are everywhere in Smallville. They're pretty, but, well . . . they're also pretty worthless." Maybe he'd been wrong about this gift, he thought, wishing he'd bought her emeralds instead.

But Lilia's smile chased his fears away. "Maybe so," she said, taking the bracelet out of the box and slipping it on her wrist. "But these, at least, are worth something to me." Lex, who had always prided himself on maintaining a cool, confident exterior, felt his heart melt a little.

☙ ☙ ☙ ☙

Lex stood by Lilia's car as she climbed inside. "You sure I can't persuade you to come back over to my place for dinner?" he asked. "We could make up for the other night."

"I'd like to, but I can't," she said, trying to rev the car. "Clark forgot one of his books in my classroom, and I thought I'd drop it off at the Kent Farm on my way home. And after that I have a ton of homework to grade." She turned the key in the ignition, but again the motor failed to turn over. "Darn this thing," she said, frustrated.

Lex looked at the beat-up car. "I think this antique may have seen better days, Lilia."

"No, it has to start . . ." She tried again. Nothing.

Lex opened her door. "Ms. Sanchez, it would be my pleasure to drive you to Clark's house and then home. Besides, I wouldn't trust this thing to get you anywhere safely. Especially with the weather," Lex said, looking up at some gathering clouds. "They say there's a bad storm coming this afternoon."

Lilia smiled and climbed out of the car. "*Gracias, Señor* Luthor," she said.

❧ ❧ ❧ ❧

As Lex and Lilia drove along the road that led to Clark's house, the sky, which had just been overcast an hour ago, turned ominously dark. Rumbling, angry-looking clouds rolled quickly in, and wind whipped the trees. "Wow," Lex said, "this looks impressive." At that moment, a bolt of lightning illuminated the sky, followed by a scary crack of thunder. Buckets of rain came down, pelting the windshield; it was difficult to see.

"*Tempestad,*" Lilia whispered, as rain beat threateningly hard against the windshield. Lex looked over at her. "It means *storm* in Spanish," she said.

"I think we might need a stronger word than that," Lex said, watching as the road began to flood.

❦ ❦ ❦ ❦

Clark came into the house soaked to the skin. "Wow, that's some storm out there," he said, not realizing his mom was on the phone. "Dad, I locked up the barn good and tight." Jonathan nodded as he closed the storm windows.

"All right, I'll have him call if he comes by," Martha said before hanging up the phone. "That was Lex's butler," she said to Clark. "He wanted to know if Lex had come here."

Clark looked confused. "He was headed over here?"

"Well, he said Lex mentioned that he was taking a drive over to the high school. The butler said he tried to reach Lex to tell him about the storm warnings — lightning struck a pool shed on their property, and some of the roads are flooding — but Lex's cell phone doesn't seem to be working. He figured Lex might have come here to take shelter."

"That's funny, I didn't see Lex around the school . . . ," Clark said. Then he realized why. "He probably went there to see Ms. Sanchez." Clark felt a twinge of jealousy, and then sadness that his friend felt he had to sneak around him to see someone he liked. *He didn't want to rub it in my face*, Clark thought. Then, a more serious thought came to him as his mother said, "I hope they're not out there in that."

Clark looked outside, but he could barely see anything because of the heavy rain lashing against the windows. A thunderbolt struck, making the house shudder.

CHAPTER 14

"Do you think we should go to your house instead?" Lilia suggested, an edge of nervousness creeping into her voice.

Lex thought for a moment, trying to steady the steering wheel without it being too noticeable. He had slowed down somewhat, but the car was still hydroplaning; the rain had quickly turned the road into a stream, and water rushed at them. "Well, we are closer to my place than to the Kent Farm," Lex said, trying to hide his concern. "Don't worry, we'll —"

"Lex, look out!" Lilia shouted.

Lex turned to look out the window on his side in time to see a wave of muddy water sliding down a hill. In it were small trees and rocks, all heading straight for the car. He stepped on the gas pedal to try to outrun it. The car fishtailed, and then the wall of mud was upon them, pushing them sideways. The road seemed to give way beneath them.

The last thing Lex heard before feeling a sharp pain — *crack!* — on the side of his head was the sound of Lilia screaming.

❦ ❦ ❦ ❦

"Clark, you're not going out in that," Jonathan Kent said firmly. But Clark was already headed toward the door. He'd called the school to see if Lex and Ms. Sanchez were there. Her car was, but Lex's wasn't, and they were nowhere to be found.

"Dad, I have to," he said. "They might be out there. Nothing's going to happen to me, but if they're stuck on the road somewhere, there's no telling what could happen to them." Jonathan sighed and nodded. He knew his son was making sense, though he still worried.

Martha also knew that there was practically

nothing that could hurt her son, yet she took his arm for a second. "Clark — just please be careful," she said.

"I will, Mom," he assured her, giving her a quick hug. When he opened the door, the wind was so strong it pushed Martha back, and Jonathan had to lean hard against the door to shut it after him. Martha looked out the window as her son became a speeding blur, followed by a plume of water.

❦ ❦ ❦

Even with her hands over her ears, Lilia could still hear the thunder, the angry pelting rain on the hood of the car. When she opened her eyes, what she saw made her breath catch in her throat.

To her left was Lex, unconscious, bleeding from the place where his head had hit the driver's-side window. The window was smashed open, and mud and water were flowing into the car, filling the bottom fast.

To her right, directly outside her caved-in door,

was a huge tree. The car had been pushed by the mud slide against the tree trunk, which, Lilia could now see, was on the edge of what looked like a crater in the earth.

Dios mío, she thought. *I'm here again. We're by the pond where the meteorites hit.*

Memories of the meteorite shower came back to her. And she'd come here the day she and Lex had met, when she was looking at the fields. They'd been so beautiful then; now they were a raging torrent of mud.

"Lex," she said urgently. "Lex, wake up!" But he was slumped in his seat, now waist-deep in the watery mud that filled the car. Lilia reached over to push his head back, afraid he would drown in the rushing water.

I will not panic, she thought. *Cell phone. Got to get help.* Holding Lex's head up with one hand, she kicked her shoes off against the car floor and searched with her feet for her purse. Her cell phone was in there, and if by some miracle it was still dry . . .

Nothing. Her purse must have been thrown

somewhere else in the car during the crash and was now lost in the mud. She didn't dare undo her seat belt to look for it — the car was too precariously pinned against the tree, and any sudden movement could cause it to shift and be pushed down the slope.

The mud in the car rose up to her neck. Lilia fought to control her breath, to stay calm. She felt along the armrest of the mangled car door for the power-window control. Somehow, it still worked; the windows opened, and mud poured out, getting down to chest level again. At least they wouldn't drown in the car.

Her relief lasted only a second before the car shifted with a creak. The rushing water, eroding the ground beneath them, was loosening the tree.

At that point, Lilia did the only thing she could. She began to scream.

"Help! Somebody, anybody! *Help us!*"

The roar of thunder drowned out her voice.

CHAPTER 15

Clark had run this fast in heavy rain before, when he was a kid, because it was fun to go into a baseball slide at sixty miles an hour. Now he was intent on keeping his footing however he could. He scanned the horizon for Lex's silver Porsche.

Lex would have stuck to the road. He might have pulled over to the side when he saw how bad the storm was getting. Clark followed the road closely, looking to both sides. He had to stop a few times because the rain was coming down so hard that he could barely see more than a few feet in front of him.

Clark ran farther down the road, which dipped at one point. Just ahead was the mud hole he'd fallen into the day he and Lex had argued. It was the last place in the world he wanted to be, with that giant meteorite at the bottom.

But there at the edge of it was Lex's car, pinned against a big tree that was now leaning diagonally. Mud and water rushed at the other side, pushing against the car. At that moment, Clark heard Lilia screaming.

🦀 🦀 🦀 🦀

"Clark!" Lilia said breathlessly. "Clark, thank God! Lex is hurt — get him out of here!"

Clark had to stop himself from ripping the car door off its hinges. It would have been so easy for him to do, but so hard to explain to Lilia and Lex how he had done it. Instead, he blocked the torrent of muddy water with his body and opened the door. Lilia reached over and undid Lex's seatbelt, and Clark pulled him free and out of the car.

Clark had to find someplace to put Lex where he wouldn't drown or get washed away. There was a boulder a few yards away up the hill, and Clark propped his friend against it.

"Clark!" Lilia's voice was a sharp cry of panic.

Clark looked over his shoulder and saw that the car was now slowly sliding, back end first, into the mud hole. Taking Lex out had shifted the balance. Lilia was still inside, about to be washed away.

He sped back to the car, getting there in less than the blink of an eye. He held the car with one hand and reached into it with the other. "Lilia!" he called, "grab onto me!"

Cautiously, she reached for Clark's outstretched hand. In his panic, Clark didn't see the green stones in the bracelet on Lilia's wrist begin to glow. He reached for her and grabbed her wrist.

The pain shot through his arm, then his whole body. For a second he thought he'd been struck by lightning. But even lightning didn't hurt like this.

NO! Clark's mind screamed. *Meteorites* —

His gasp became a shout of agony.

ಇ ಇ ಇ ಇ

Clark clenched his teeth, trying to keep from screaming. But he still heard someone screaming . . .

It was Lilia.

Clark could hardly breathe because of the pain shooting through his hand from the bracelet on Lilia's wrist. It cut through his entire body, making his veins throb like they were going to explode right under his skin. Then he looked at Lilia, whose face was also twisted in suffering. He didn't understand — nothing had happened to her. But it became clear a second later when Lilia's mouth opened and Clark's thoughts came gushing out of her in a torrent.

"No, no, no, it hurts, it hurts! The meteorites, no, please stop. I'm dying. No, no, can't let them see me like this; they'll know, they'll know the truth about me. It hurts. Have to let go, can't let go, have to LET GO —"

Clark was horrified. The pain he was feeling was bad enough, but the fear that Lex might hear what Lilia was saying . . . there would be no way to explain this. At that moment, he heard moaning behind him. He turned to see Lex coming slowly back to life.

Clark's foot slipped underneath him, and he fell to the ground. His strength was failing, being sucked out of him by the meteorites on Lilia's wrist. He could barely breathe, could barely hold on to the car. In another second, it would slide down the slope.

I can't let her go, Clark thought. *But I've got to.* And at that second, he did.

☙ ☙ ☙ ☙

In a superspeed blur, Clark released his grip on Lilia's arm, but not before he grabbed the bracelet and pulled it off her wrist. The touch of the meteorites burned scalding pain into his hand . . . and then the bracelet fell from his hand into the rushing water. Clark saw it wash right out the window behind Lilia.

Instantly, Clark felt his strength return. In a flash, he jumped back to his feet, braced them firmly against the slick ground, and took hold of Lilia's wrist again.

"Lilia!" Clark yelled over the sound of thunder, trying to bring her out of her wooziness. "Your seat belt!"

Lilia shook her head clear, reached down into

the mud for the seat belt clasp, and freed herself. Clark pulled her out of the car and onto the ground, where he kept an arm protectively around her. She was turned away from him so she didn't see him let go of Lex's car. There was a cracking noise as the tree finally gave way, and the car slid down the slope, turning upside down as it fell. The mud rushed up to it, coming up almost to the tires. Clark carried Lilia up the hill and away from the mud slide, where they both collapsed on the ground.

As he watched the mud cover the car, Clark used his X-ray vision to scan the bottom of the crater. No sign of the meteor rocks, even the huge one that had almost killed him. They'd all been washed away by the storm.

His sigh of relief was echoed by Lilia, who gently closed her eyes and let her head rest on Clark's shoulder. He felt the slight dizziness from the meteorite flecks inside her; even still, he allowed himself, just for a moment, to hold her in his arms, to feel her pressed against him. Then they got to their feet and went to take care of Lex.

CHAPTER 16

The next day, Clark was sitting in the Beanery coffee bar just as Lex was walking by. He tapped on the window and motioned for Lex to come inside.

"I'm surprised to see you here," Lex said as he sat down in an armchair next to Clark. "Don't you usually hang out at the Talon?"

"I think I needed a change of scenery," Clark said, not wanting to get into the whole Whitney-and-Lana story. "Apparently so did Ms. Sanchez. Mr. Hector was back at school today, a week early."

Lex nodded. "Lilia called before she left to see how I was," he said, touching the bandage on the side of his forehead. "She told me she was going back to Madrid. Even she had to admit that after one meteor shower, one scaffolding collapse, and one mud slide, this town seems to be bad luck for her." Lex managed a weak smile, then sighed and looked out the window.

Clark felt bad for his friend. For all the money Lex had, he seemed to have nothing but disappointment in his life — his terrible relationship with his dad, his bad reputation in Smallville, and now, it seemed, Lex was unlucky in love too. Clark hoped that Lex would eventually find something in his life that would make him happy. These constant frustrations could really make a guy become bitter and twisted someday.

"I almost forgot," said Lex, turning back to Clark. "Lilia wanted me to tell you something."

"What was it?"

"She said, 'Don't keep what's in your heart a buried secret. If you keep your heart open, then love will come to you.'" Lex paused. "She said you'd know what it meant."

Clark let Lilia's words sink in. It was her gift to him, and he hoped he'd come to understand it in time.

He looked at Lex's downcast expression. "Can I buy you a latte?" Clark said.

Lex smiled. "Make it a double."

❧ ❧ ❧ ❧

Clark was in the hayloft in the barn, sitting by his telescope, not looking through it but just staring into space. What was that song his mom sang sometimes? *What a difference a day makes.* Yesterday, the sky had been as dark as iron, rain had lashed the land, and floods had washed over everything. Today, the sun was out, and the day had been beautiful. Yesterday, he could barely think about anything but a woman who had almost come between him and a close friend; today, she was headed back to Spain, he and Lex were friends again, and everything was back to normal.

Almost.

Clark smiled when he heard the familiar footsteps coming up the stairs, recognizing the sound instantly: Lana. He turned, and there she was,

146

standing tentatively at the top of the wooden steps.

"Hey," she said, waiting to see Clark's reaction. When it turned out to be a big welcoming smile, she stepped toward him.

"You're just in time," Clark said, gesturing toward the setting sun. The sky was splashed with orange and laced with purple clouds. "And we've got the best seats in the house." Lana sat next to him, mentally breathing a sigh of relief.

They sat in a comfortable quiet for a moment or two. Then, Lana said, "Clark . . . I know things have been . . . well, a little weird between us lately. But I just want you to know —"

Clark reached over and took Lana's hand. "I know," he said. He smiled at her, and she smiled back, giving his hand a gentle squeeze. He couldn't help noticing there was no ring on her finger, but he didn't want to ruin the moment by asking her what had happened. He would find out in time.

It was then that Clark finally understood that secret language of the eyes that his parents

shared. It happened when you were with someone who understood you completely, even if only
for that moment. You might not know everything about each other, and you might not know
what was going to happen in the future, but for
that moment . . . *Everything is just the way it should
be right now*, Clark thought. *It's perfect.*

"Hey, we're missing the best part," Lana said,
looking toward the setting sun.

"No way," Clark said, still holding Lana's hand.
"It's all the best part."

About the Author

Suzan Colón is the author of *Catwoman: The Life and Times of a Feline Fatale*. She has worked as an editor and written feature articles for many magazines, including *Mademoiselle*, *Jane*, and *Latina*. She lives in New York City.